THE DECEIT BIRDS

GAVIN EYERS

Best wishes

Gavin Eyers

27/11/17

Printed by CreateSpace, an Amazon.com company

This book is dedicated to my family

ONE

I am in my car.

My knees are in front of my face. My arms are pinned to my sides. Fists clenched. I'm out of breath and trembling. Blood is rushing to my head and my eyelid twitches. I can smell petrol. My hearing has become suddenly, impeccably clear. Yelling. My neck is stiff as I turn my head, very gently, and see the world upside down through where the window has been smashed out. A woman is yelling. From my position I can only see her shoes, as she rushes, clip-clopping, towards me. They stop beside my face. She kneels on the road and peers in at me, looking panicked.

'Are you hurt?'

I felt an impact, but I feel no pain. It was so sudden. I don't know what happened. My car rolled as many times as it wanted to. I wasn't in control by then. And now I'm wrapped in metal.

'Can you move?'

The woman takes off her jacket and places it over the jagged edges of the window. She holds my hand. I slowly edge sideways through the hole in the window, until she grips me under my arms and pulls. I see my legs appear from the wreckage. I can move them.

I lie back on the road, look up and cry out, enormously relieved at the sight of the morning sky.

I stand and run my hands over my arms and legs. They ache just a little, like I've woken from a long and deep sleep. I spit, spit and spit onto the road, expecting to see blood or something of the bitter taste in my mouth, but all I see are splatters of nothing amongst broken glass and plastic and metal, bits of I don't know what. I look down and see glass littering my shirt and trousers. Then, cutting through the smell of the petrol, I get a faint hint of the vanilla-scented water that Mia sprays on our clothes as she irons them. I try to take a deep breath of it, but the petrol cuts through again.

No blood soaks through my clothes and I don't hurt anywhere. I feel my face for wetness, my chests, my thighs. Nothing. I press all over my body to find pain but find none. I think I banged my head. I'm dizzy.

'Are you OK?' The pretty woman in her thirties with long mahogany hair looks at me – my face then body, body then face. She holds my hand, and touches my cheek with intimate delicacy. We look each other in the eyes as if we've just kissed.

'I think I am.' She puts her hand on my back, guides me to the side of the road, and I sit on the kerb. 'I don't know what happened.'

People are standing in their doorways, wearing night clothes. Others look out from pulled back curtains. I look down the road towards home. It's too far away for Mia to have heard the bang and crunch of my car.

A man with grey hair and a tired face, dressed in a suit, stands in front of me.

'I think I banged my head.'

He rubs his hands through my hair but finds no cuts or blood. As he bends down and speaks to me, his tie falls in front of my face and I focus on it, black with a tint of blue, like a magpie's back.

'I can't see any injury, but I'll call an ambulance anyway just in case. And the police. Can I call anyone else for you?' He has pale eyes. He speaks quickly and looks more shocked than I feel.

'No.' I need to leave before the police arrive.

I look in my cupped hands at my mobile phone, which had somehow exited the car. A teenage girl wearing a bright pink jumper has gathered the pieces and handed them to me, but it will never talk again.

I don't want to tell Mia about the accident over the phone anyway. She'll panic. I imagine her eyes opening wide and her hand grabbing for her mouth, her heart beating as fast as mine is now. She'll be lying, stretched amongst the white sheets of our bed now, lost in sleep. I can't bear the thought of dragging her from that place to this.

'He thinks he banged his head,' the man says.

Carl will be at home, sleeping too. He said he'd drive Mia to the garden centre later, as they've both got the day off work and I've taken the car. If they hadn't taken the day off, one or both of them might have been in the car with me, and I look at the shattered pieces of phone in my cupped hands, feeling fortunate. I don't want to tell Carl over the phone either. I know him as I know myself. Though he won't show panic on the outside, it will shake him from the inside. I'll walk home and tell them about the car.

'I'm going to walk home. It's only a few minutes away.' I point towards home to the strangers.

'But I've already called the police. I think you should wait for them to get here,' the man says.

The girl in the pink jumper hasn't said anything to me, but relays everything to someone on her phone. 'His car is smashed! Absolute mash-up! And the bloke ain't got a scratch on him!'

She looks at me as if I can't hear her.

I see a little dog sitting on the opposite side of the road.

A little terrier thing with long eyebrows and a beard like an old man, his head slightly tilted to one side, as if listening. It has an expression of sympathy, doesn't take its eyes off mine.

The man and woman are talking to each other, saying that they need to stay as witnesses.

'I saw the whole thing,' the woman says.

'But I don't know what happened.'

'It's all right,' the man says. 'You probably just lost control of the car.'

The woman nods.

Across the road, the dog has gone.

I look at my car. It's upside down and its roof is crushed. Its windows lie shattered in crystals all over the road, sparkling in the early morning light. There's no space I can see inside my car that a person might fit into. I don't know how I climbed out.

'I'm going to walk home,' I say again. I stand and brush my hands down the front of my shirt. My belt buckle and shoes still shine. My grey silk tie is too low. Someone has loosened it. It's tangled in my work security pass. *Lewis Brown. Administration Manager.*

I feel calmer for having left the accident. It's nearly full daylight now, but the early kind where not much life is going on. Birds are singing and curtains are being yanked open, but the only person I can see now is a muscular man who I often see jogging when I'm leaving for work. He nods good morning to me. I don't think he has any idea that something might be wrong.

I see my house. My home. Light carpets on the floors and pictures on the walls. A gentle smell of coffee in the kitchen. All these things are half mine and I cherish them. The curtains are closed and I realise again that they'll still be sleeping. Mia lying stretched amongst the white sheets, patches of skin exposed to the October morning air, her beautiful dark hair spread on the pillows. Carl in the box room, covered with the duvet like a tortoise under his shell. Hiding and hidden. He always sleeps in tangled positions. My best friend. I know everything there is to know about him.

I stand in front of the hallway mirror. My face is pale, as if my blood is clear and my eyes look like they have a thin layer of ice over them. My breathing speeds up again, but I manage to control it this time. I rub my hand over my head. There's a pain on my forehead now and a slight swelling. I pass my finger across it. It feels warm. I'm still alive.

I walk upstairs, feel the smoothness of the carpet under my shoes. The door to the box room is open a little. I stand on the landing for a moment, deciding which of them I should wake first. Then I go to the door of the front bedroom. It's slightly open too. Everything is still. I compose myself for waking her.

I hear a strong, finger-burn gasp. It makes me jump. I turn my head and listen hard, my ear towards the opening of the door. I don't want to make Mia jump too. She'll not be expecting anyone to walk in. I take a breath to clear my throat, give her a warning signal, but as soon as my breath is inside me it stops because I hear a moan. A nightmare moan. A sound you make when your dreams are so bad that you try to drag yourself back to consciousness, call out loud to wake yourself. Mia has nightmares sometimes and hits out and kicks in her sleep. She doesn't remember them when she wakes. I hate seeing her in distress and gently try to wake her, though I'm sure there's a saying that says you shouldn't wake someone who is having a nightmare. I don't know why though, so I try to wake her with reassuring words.

I hear a cry, uncontrolled and desperate, like a man kicked in the balls, but the cry came from Mia. I know this sound. My breathing starts again, so powerfully that I feel an instant bulge in my throat and I remember the little dog on the other side of the road, its expression of sympathy. He looked at me as if my life had just ended.

I push the door, exposing a line of vision into the room.

Mia's legs. Carl's back.

Unable to move or make a sound, I watch them. Until her eyes glimpse mine.

Mia screams.

TWO

Staring at the floor, I sit on the end of the bed opposite a full-length mirror that I can't bear to look into. My arms feel like I have swum for a day, my legs like I have run through a night. I can't lift my head straight. I had a cool shower at some point, maybe days ago, and never thought to dress again. I don't remember checking into the hotel.

My gaze drifts from the floor to my legs, which rest close to each other, knees almost touching. The hair on them looks weak and gleams from the sheet of light cast through a gap in the curtains. I forget the horror, and then it rushes back and my gaze drops to the floor.

How could she let him touch her? My knees fall against each other, hands stretched either side of me, gripping the edge of the bed for balance. I can't begin to gather the feelings of loss.

I sit in the hotel room because I don't know where to go or what to do. I don't think I could hit Carl, not even now. I don't think I could yell at Mia either. I never have in the fourteen years since we met. I heard them yell at each other as I walked down the path after discovering them. Mia's voice was high and panicked. Carl's was his usual voice, only loud. If me and Mia have never yelled at each other, how could Mia and Carl? It must be part of this world they share. A world in which I don't exist.

My chest hurts. My throat feels as thin as a straw, throbs when I breathe or swallow. My eyes are wide open, as if alerted to danger, but there's only the floor, the picture in my mind, my memories of everything good being brushed with nettles. I see Mia's hair damp with sweat. I see their ankles entwined over each other.

I move to the floor. The wiry carpet threatens to graze my back as I watch the line of light under the door. The carpet is littered with my clothes, a white towel from the bathroom and the plastic packet from two biscuits covered in sugar and dotted with raisins that had been on the desk next to the kettle. My stomach hurt so much that I thought they'd help and I ate them. They felt like gravel in my throat when they came back up a few minutes later. It's dark now. Day passed into night without my noticing. There is little light in the room, a reddish glow from the TV standby, a little beam through the gap in the curtains from the night outside, which can have no moon, but I'm watching the line of light. I am anchored to it.

What would have happened if I'd not run down the stairs and away when Mia screamed?

I see Carl. He can't look me in the eye for longer than a few seconds as he lays there naked, his hands cupped between his legs. He looks at me, then Mia, then back at me, like he's been accused of something he knows nothing about. Behind that faked expression I can see his eyes about to burst with tears. A throat about to choke with shock. Mia just holds her hand over her mouth and makes a sort of sobbing sound, though I don't think she cries. She can't take her eyes off mine. I ran down the stairs, so I'll never know.

I see shadows walk past the line of light, hear voices in the corridor. *Do Not Disturb* has warned people for days, except for when I have ordered room service drinks and then they have knocked gently, though I don't know how many times I have ordered, or how many days I've been here. I haven't slept yet that I know of.

I don't know when I lay on the floor, or why. I have my boxer shorts on now. I'm not cold, though the air is cool and my chest tingles. I bring my hand up to it, then down over my body. Every time my fingers pass over any part of me, it hurts, makes me wince. I see Mia's hand gripping the bedframe, her wedding band gold and shining. I see a look of hunger on Carl's face. I see him reading words from her closed eyes.

I feel it coming again and roll over onto my knees. My breath shortens, like I've been kicked in the stomach. I forget everything, get up and stumble into the bathroom, fall onto my knees. My hands grip cold white porcelain. I retch and retch. My body makes me do it, like it's rejecting something poisonous I've ingested. My stomach contracts. My back spasms. My throat tightens from all the whisky I've gulped neat since arriving at the hotel. There's nothing left to come out but still I retch. My knees hurt against the tiled floor but there's nothing I can do to end it, until eventually my body decides it has tried enough for now and I can breathe again, painfully and gratefully. I open my eyes and see the toilet bowl, a faint silhouette of my head in the still water.

I lean back against the bath and wrap my hands around my legs, try to hold my body together, stop it from falling apart, until my breathing slows.

THREE

I stand in the hotel lobby after waking up on the floor of my room. I don't know how long I was asleep. It might have been a day and a night. It might have been two of each.

Movement, people, voices surround me. Laughing children run. Lift doors open and close and bleep. Music plays softly, though I have no idea which direction it comes from. It just hangs in the air. I don't remember how much my room was going to cost and have no idea what the person looked like who gave me the key card that I now grip in my hand.

An elderly couple stand at the reception desk, checking out. They're taking forever to do so, talking in detail about the service they've received to the girl behind the desk, who clearly couldn't give a shit, but still they tell her. After finally receiving a receipt for their cash, they thank the girl profusely. Then the man takes the woman's hand as they walk away and he pulls their heavy-looking suitcase with his other hand. I watch them until they go through the automatic doors and step out into London.

'Can I help you?'

I look up. The girl has a false smile. As I walk closer to the desk I see that it is more than false, it's bordering on nasty. She's a fraud. I don't like her. I ask to check out, hand her my key card, and she taps at her computer for a moment then looks at me, expressionless. I think her smile has run out. I wonder what she's going to say, what she thinks of me. I have no luggage and I stand in the clothes I was wearing when I was in my upside-down car.

'Five nights, no breakfasts. That's £550, plus a £240 drinks bill. That's £790 please.' She takes my debit card and places it into the machine.

It asks me for my PIN, and a feeling of panic goes through me. The girl is busy typing things into her computer again. I look back down at the little screen and its question for me. I type in the number and press *enter* and the machine bleeps loudly and tells me my answer was incorrect. The girl looks up for a moment. I try to concentrate. I feel so tired, so hungry, so sick. My finger reaches up again and types four digits. I don't know where they come from. I press *enter* and it tells me *OK.*

I pick up a free ads newspaper from a rack next to the reception desk and begin to look for cheaper hotels and then for rooms to rent. I need to get out of here. I want to lie on my sofa, lie in my bed, make myself something to eat in the kitchen to stop my stomach from hurting the way it does, but I know I can't. I want to see Mia, have my breakfast with her. We often have our breakfast in the garden. After, I sit and read the papers. Mia walks around as soon as she has finished eating, doing the jobs she had spotted while we ate. She might prune the bushes, fill the bird feeders or feed the fish in the pond, and I'm always more interested in watching her than reading anything in the papers. She has always been a distraction to me. I could watch her for hours. I want to be sitting in the garden and for her to ask me how I'm coping, what she can do to help.

Prices, addresses, availability. Normal things, but they

take effort and life I don't feel I have. I read names of places I recognise but straight away rule out. Too posh there, too hectic there, too much trouble there. Shared kitchen, non-smoker preferred, must like cats. To share a bathroom with four others, eight minutes from the Tube, own sink in room. Homes and lives described in a few words and a price, including or excluding bills. I circle a few places and then call their numbers from a payphone in the hotel lobby.

I leave the hotel and breathe fresh air, or fresh London air, and head towards the river. I want to look into it. I walk through Jubilee Gardens and towards The Eye, watching over London. People in business dress pass me. It must be a weekday. Tourists too, so many tourists, happy and calling to one another, pointing things out, standing in groups for photographs and smiling. Carefree moments. I feel I'll never have one again, the weight on my mind is so overwhelming, and when I think about it more I'm not even sure if I want one again. I no longer want to be in the huddle. Mia won't be in it with me anyway. I'll take the pictures.

At the river wall, I look at the buildings opposite. Grey and sparkling.

London.

Though I've lived here for twelve years, I've never felt like a Londoner. Most of what I know about this city, I've seen on TV. The rave clubs and the seedy clubs, the arts and the artists, the never-ending mix of lives and lifestyles. I hear Big Ben boom at midday and look across the river to it. Even in this dark moment, standing at this spot and seeing the city makes me feel a little burst of life, even though it feels pointless and bitter and mad.

I rest my elbows on the wall and look down. The tide is out and a little muddy beach is exposed. Seagulls jump around each other. They try to scare each other away from a little silver eel-like thing one of them must have pulled from the river. The eel slithers and squirms and wriggles on the stones and mud. It fights and fights but it doesn't stand a chance really. It gets snatched in a beak and swallowed alive.

Even at low tide the river looks strong, travelling along its path and making London live around it. I've always loved the river and need to travel down it a few miles now. I could get a train, but the river seems somehow more direct. A clearer journey. I walk towards Festival Pier.

The other passengers are mainly tourists, again, but there are still a few business types in suits. The water is calm, but as we leave the pier and head east, the boat bounces and makes my stomach turn. My stomach has had no food for five days, other than the biscuits, which didn't stay in there long. Then there's been the whisky. It feels tense, my stomach. Angry, and as hard as a golf ball.

I stand on the open-top deck of the boat with my arms on the railings, trying to get what I can from the October sun. It gives hardly any warmth today. I look over, into the deep and murky Thames. It's surprisingly clear of litter, and I remember an article I read once which told of the vast variety of fish that inhabit it. Two mallards bob past at speed. In the water, I see Mia gripping the back of Carl's head, as little streams of sweat roll down between his shoulders. I rub my hand across my forehead. The swelling from the car crash has almost gone now, but the place where it was feels bruised.

City Hall and Tate Modern pass on my right, St Paul's and the City on my left. A couple stand next to me, eating crisps. I smell their salt and think I must try to eat something today. Then the warehouses pass by, the factories, now all converted into flats. Chains hang from their walls. Big, closed doors drop down into the river. This kind of journey would normally excite me, but not today. Maybe today I feel more like a Londoner.

Docklands soon appears, silver and shining, towering over the river. Then, the boat docks at Greenwich. I'm nearly there now. I know where I need to go. I step off the boat, walk up the pier and look up at the Cutty Sark as I pass by.

Greenwich Market and its crowds. I remember visiting here. I was with Mia and Carl. We picked things up and talked to the stallholders about their creations, tried foods because they'd been so meticulously prepared. I slowly work my way through the buyers and sellers, feel like I'm going against the flow. There's a warm stench of beer. I breathe it deeply. I don't have time to stop now.

I walk through the big black gates of Greenwich Park and enter a beautiful place. I've not been here before, but today it feels wonderfully familiar. Green and green and green. Enormous, ancient trees. Birdsong. The scent of newly cut grass, so fresh I can taste it. A little warmth is coming through now. I feel the sun on my face, my ears, my neck, on everything it can find to shine on. I see people flying kites, soaring even though there's only a light wind. A few people are sitting on the grass. Most must be at work. I hear screeching and look up, see a flock of parakeets fly high above me. I've only ever seen them once, years ago, and wondered if I'd seen them at all and not been mistaken. Them making London home is bewildering, but they are here. They fly over me fleetingly, long tails silhouetted against the blue sky.

I climb the fierce incline towards the Observatory, which takes all the strength I can gather. When I reach it, I turn and look at the view. It is breathtaking. London looks gigantic, powerful and silent from here. After a comforting moment watching it, I continue walking through the park, following the little pathways, through rose gardens and past ponds. People walk together, a dog runs and barks excitedly and chases a squirrel until it runs up a tree trunk. A gaggle of geese argue, get louder and louder, then gradually calm down, the argument apparently settled.

On the other side of the park, I walk out of the gates. The traffic of a busy road roars in front of me. After I cross it, I stop and see Blackheath. It's mostly bare grass. A massive empty space so flat that the sky is no longer above but all around me. A few people are here, playing football, walking, jogging. There is a feeling of calmness here, and as I begin to cross the grass towards the village I feel a sense of peace, which grows as I walk, as though I'm walking into the heart of it.

On Yarrow Road, I look up at number 28. The house is a giant, too big to be a home. It stands on its own, with the dark trails from a plant, now long gone, crawling over its dirty white walls. The curtains are open in all the windows, showing emptiness where life might once have been, like the screens of switched-off televisions. Chimneys poke out all over the roof, and a small, tree-ish thing grows from the gutter. The house might be a hundred years old. Maybe two hundred. It was here when I was born and it will still be here when I die. I like houses like this. There are steps up to the front door and I walk up them, find a little white round doorbell on the left. It has a plastic rectangle next to it with *Mrs Moore* written by hand in smeared black ink. I press the bell then quickly let go, feeling that it's ice-cold on my fingertip. It makes the sound of an alarm clock, violent and clanging and loud. I wait.

I look down the side of the steps and see a pathway which goes under where I stand, cold-looking and dotted with bright green moss. There are sash windows to a basement flat. Just as I'm about to press the bell again, I see a figure through the narrow frosted pane of glass limply walking closer.

She opens the door. She is old, very old. Her movements are slow. She wears a wine-red dress with a brooch pinned above her heart, an oval of pale yellow glass with a small dragonfly set in it. Her hair is thin and tied back, jet-black. It must be dyed. Everything about her makes me think her hair should be very grey.

'Mrs Moore?'

'Hello,' she says, gently, towards the ground. She puts a hand on the doorframe for balance, then slowly looks up. Her eyes are deep and green. Green like grass after rain. Green like mine. She looks closely at my face, squints, as if trying to focus on words on a page, then after a few seconds her eyes widen, in shock at what she has just read. Her mouth opens, and as she gasps, her old hand reaches up and covers her mouth, like one might when first hearing of some amazing good fortune, or at seeing an accident and a car roll and roll and roll.

'Dear God.' Her eyes are filled with tears.

I think she might be mad.

'I'm Lewis.'

She looks frighteningly confused, like she's trying to find the answer for a question I haven't asked her. The silence goes on for longer than I can possibly be comfortable with. I can hardly look at her. I put my hands in my pockets, trying to hide my discomfort in there with them. I take a step backwards, need to walk away from this, but seeing my retreat, she speaks.

'You must come in.'

The hallway is long and dull in the light from the frosted pane of the closing door. A little more light comes from the far end of the hallway, through a slightly open door at the back of the house. Halfway down the hall is a fireplace, neither lit nor cleaned out since it was last used. The smell of ashes reminds me of my parent's house. The air tastes earthy. There's a stillness within the house, like silence has replaced some other entity, long gone. The house feels dead other than for Mrs Moore, who now looks at me expectantly. The hall is silent except for her gentle breaths. She still looks shaken.

'Has Patrick brought you here?' She asks, in almost a whisper.

I feel closed in now, trapped in this mad woman's house. I shouldn't have walked through the door.

'I don't know anyone called Patrick.'

She shakes her head, though she doesn't take her eyes off mine.

'I can see him.' She puts her hand to my cheek and I flinch from her cold, waxy fingers.

She lowers her hand and rests it on her stomach with her other hand, as if praying over the place where a child might once have grown. I try to think of a reason why I can leave this house and get away from her, but she speaks before I can think of anything.

'The rooms on the top floor of the house are still liveable, if you need somewhere to stay. I've not been up there for a while.'

I see someone walk across the other end of the hallway, just glimpsing them as they pass from one door through another.

'How many people live here?'

'Just me here.'

She moves slowly past me, to the bottom of the stairs.

'Do you have someone visiting then?'

She concentrates on her feet.

'You don't need to go up the stairs if you are not able to.' I feel awkward for the effort she is making. 'I can look for somewhere else to stay.'

She takes the first step. I give her a moment to get ahead and then I walk behind, ready to catch her if she falls back. Some of her neatly tied-back hair has loosened. It sways next to her ear with each step. Her hair is cut the length that would suit a young woman but her movements are old and mechanical. She climbs the steps one at a time, placing both feet on the same step and looking up before she puts a hand on her knee and attempts the next. I hope she doesn't feel any pain.

At the top of the stairs we walk slowly along a landing, bright from a large window at the front of the house. I see the heath through it. All the doors on the landing are slightly open, but I see nothing but bareness in the rooms.

Another staircase. The house is enormous. Mrs Moore appears to be speeding up a little, though she is still slow. On the next landing, she rests for a moment and I expect her to begin showing me around.

'One more,' she says, nodding towards a narrower staircase.

We emerge onto a small landing then go into a living room that smells of flowers or perfume and has only a sofa, which might once have been white. The bedroom is empty except for a metal bedframe and a mattress with a small folded blanket on it. The kitchen looks equipped and the bathroom bare. All the rooms have a fireplace, except the kitchen. One final room is empty. I've seen no carpet other than the thin strip up the middle of the staircases. Just floorboards everywhere. It's like they're holding the house together.

'I have money. How much is the deposit?'

'No need.' Mrs Moore looks at my face closely again. 'The house is getting damp. There's a fireplace in most rooms. Throw a log in them as you pass. There's plenty in the shed.'

I still haven't said if I want to move in but she has assumed I will.

Of course, I want to live here.

'But how much is the rent?'

For a few seconds, she just looks at me, her initial shock at meeting me beginning to subside.

'I live in the basement flat. It's a big house, so do as you please. I used to run it as a boarding house, many years ago, so I'm familiar with people being here. There's a key for the front door on one of the tables, somewhere.'

She puts her hand on my arm. At first I think it's for balance, but she's looking into my eyes again. I don't know what she's looking for. It makes me nervous and I pull away very gently, then pretend it was to straighten out my shirt, which I've been wearing for so many days it's creased and smells sweaty and of something I don't even recognise.

'Lewis?'

My throat is dry. I suddenly struggle to speak.

'Yes?'

'I'll leave you to rest now. You look like you need it.'

I'm embarrassed at what she thinks I look like. I hope she can't smell my shirt. She walks to the top of the stairs and I walk over to her.

'Let me help you down,' I say, offering her my arm to link onto hers.

She waves it away. 'I'm used to coping on my own.'

As she slowly begins to descend the stairs, I go to my new bedroom. I sit on the floor with my back against the cold metal bedframe, listening to her slow footsteps, one by one, as they fade within the house. When the footsteps stop, a door slams and one in my mind opens. Like I've just woken here unexpectedly, I look at the room around me, at the bare walls, the dirty window, the door I don't remember closing. On the floorboards are clumps of dust, and beside me a dead moth with a ripped wing. For a moment I can't remember getting here then slowly I remember the heath, the parakeets, the river, the eel, the hotel and, days ago, Mia's scream.

The first drops of the flood drip from my eyes, run down my cheeks and tap onto the floorboards.

FOUR

Me and Carl would lie with our arms and legs wrapped around the long branches hanging low over the edge of the lake. Gripping tight, very still. We were young. Eight years old, maybe less, when we started doing it. We'd spend most summer evenings hugging the branches and looking down into the shallow water, talking quietly, watching the fish.

Pike waited motionless, like thin grey pipes, and snatched their prey as it passed. Perch chased around little fish like a cat might chase a butterfly. Carp would feed from the muddy lake bed, their tails flapping gently out of the water's surface like soft wet fans, and brown tench passed under us slowly, sulkily. Shoals of roach would speed by like the reflections of flocks of birds flying above us. It was the golden tench we were looking for, though, to see how they fed. We guessed there were less than ten in the whole lake, and our mission was to catch one.

As dusk began to fall, we'd hear the distant shriek of a whistle. Mum telling us it was time to start making our way home through the woods.

'That was your mum blowing the whistle,' Carl would

whisper from his branch.

'Five more minutes.'

We lived near the village of Whiteflower in West Sussex. The village was small, calm, had a red phone box beside the church that people passing through would stop and have their photo taken next to. There was one shop with a Post Office counter. The pub, The Pheasant, had carpets smelling of beer, yellowed ceilings and stuffed animals in glass cases on shelves. Nothing much happened in Whiteflower. It was peaceful. There was one road in and one road out. A couple of miles outside the village was a turning off this road, leading into the thick Whiteflower Woods, and there, at the end of a lane with no name, our houses stood side by side, joined by their coal sheds.

We'd both lived there all our lives.

Our houses were built of red brick and had old metal window frames which let too much cold through in the winter. The floorboards squeaked like excited mice. Each house had three bedrooms. Carl had the tiny room on the back of his house. Our tiny room, as I was the only child in our house, was Dad's office. He had a desk under the window and would sit there and look things up in his thick dictionary, and he was always writing letters, though I can't imagine he had many to respond to. Maybe just bills. When my Great Aunt Ruth came to stay, as she often did, especially in summer, the desk would be moved out and the little camp bed brought down from the loft and unfolded with its tight, screeching springs. I used to imagine it snapping shut and folding her flat like a deckchair one night as she slept. I told her this once and she laughed so hard that she spilled tea from her cup. She was Dad's aunt. We were always close. I'd go and stay with her, and I think the only reason she came and stayed at our house was to spend time with me. Whenever I think of that house, it reminds me of her and of how we used to laugh.

Most rooms in our house had a fireplace. The grates in

the bedrooms were small, just big enough for one thick log and a lump or two of coal. I was only allowed to light the fire in my bedroom on the coldest of winter nights. The sight of its flicker and its red glow kept me warmer than the fire itself. I would watch it from my bed with the blankets wrapped around my head, only my face feeling the cool air.

The surfaces in the house were covered in ornaments. Mum had hundreds of them. She would buy them for pennies at car boot sales, and relatives and friends would bring her one or two back from their holidays and pay her with them if she did them a good turn. Brass animals, glass stars and flowers, crystal shapes which threw rainbow colours on the walls when the sun shone through them. China figures. A man holding a spade. A lady with a parasol. Three wooden children playing flutes. Clocks, tiny clocks everywhere. She would go around the house checking their times as she dusted, the scent of polish wafting from room to room.

Dad had books everywhere. Novels, biographies, guides on DIY, which he rarely did. Books about gardening, health, travel, which he never did. I shared his interest in fiction, but we had different tastes. He liked anything war-related. I liked anything that told stories about people living in big cities. Cities felt exotic, but I'd think that with all those people there in one place, all rushing past each other, that everyone must feel very lonely.

FIVE

I stand in the loft above my rooms, looking out of the little window with the big view of Blackheath. I find a sense of belonging in these mornings, looking out as daylight emerges over the heath. The sky turns from black to dark blue first, and then it slowly brightens. I watch this most mornings, as I haven't had a proper night's sleep since I found Mia and Carl tangled together.

I'm not getting used to this house though. It's so different to the home I shared with Mia. Our house in Putney is homely, with double glazing and underfloor heating. In the winter, it is warm. The road outside is quiet. Sometimes I would lie awake at night and the only thing I'd hear would be Mia's sleeping breaths.

This house doesn't sleep. The floorboards creak and crack all night, sometimes loudly, like a stone is being dropped onto them. The pipes rattle and shudder and I hear the tick-tock of a clock, though I can't find where it is. I often wake, knowing I have been woken by a sound, but unsure of what it was.

On a few occasions I've heard Mrs Moore walking

around the house at night – one time coming slowly up the three flights of stairs to where my rooms are and standing outside my bedroom door. I sat up in bed expecting her to come into the room but she didn't. At first I thought she was whispering to someone, or talking to herself, but when I listened hard I could hear some of her words. She was talking to God. I've heard her whisper to God a few times around the house since. After a few minutes she began her slow walk back down the stairs and through the bare house until I heard the door to her basement flat slam shut. I lie in bed, wondering why she was so often awake at night too and why this time she had come all the way up to my bedroom door. I remember Aunt Ruth telling me that old people never sleep well. I wish I'd asked her why.

I've somehow got used to Mrs Moore, from a distance at least. She has a caring nature. When I see her, usually as I'm going in or out of the house, she still looks at me strangely, but not as much as she did on the day I arrived. She still puts her hands on my arms or shoulders as she speaks to me and touches my face with her fingertips. At first it made me feel uncomfortable, but not now. I think it's just what she does.

I stare at the view from the little loft window and realise I've been daydreaming again. I came up here to look for anything I might be able to use, as I have only the possessions I had on me the morning I crashed my car. The clothes I was wearing, my broken mobile phone, house keys, and my wallet containing a photo of me and Mia taken by a stranger on our honeymoon. I've always carried it with me but I can't bear to see it now.

I've looked around the loft with my head bowed as the rafters are too low for me to stand at my full height, and now I kneel beside one of the closed boxes and think about opening it. They are not mine and I feel that I shouldn't open them, but it seems that no one has been up here for a very long time and I don't think Mrs Moore will notice I've been up here at all. Dust sheets cover a few small items of furniture, but other than that there are only the boxes.

I lift the flaps and see that this one is filled with books. Books of all kinds. Novels, a children's encyclopaedia, school exercise books filled with scrawly handwriting and doodles. There is no name on the covers of the exercise books, and they are covered with pictures of, I think, an eighties' singer. He doesn't look familiar, has jet-black scruffy hair, like it has just been pulled in many directions, and a face painted as white as a pigeon egg.

The next box has clothes. A young man's clothes. I pull them out and hold them up. A military-style jacket looks too small for me. A pair of black trousers, not very dissimilar to those I've been wearing for the past two weeks, look like they might fit when I stand and hold them against my front, but against my own trousers I see that those from the box are faded. I'd be better off to keep washing mine in the sink, as I did a few days ago. They have been crumpled since. I find a burgundy jumper and hold it against my chest. It needs washing. It smells of loft. I'll wash it in the sink, try to stretch it out a little and leave it to dry on the side of the bath.

I walk downstairs as I need to go into Blackheath Village. Mrs Moore is on her knees in the ground-floor hallway, cleaning out the fireplace with a bucket and brush.

'Hello, Mrs Moore,' I say, wanting to keep the conversation to a minimum.

'How are you, Lewis? You look very pale today.'

She stands and looks at my face closely. She goes to touch it but sees the soot on her fingertips and stops an inch or so from my face, then wipes her hand on her apron.

'I'm doing fine, thanks, just got a bit of a headache, that's all.' I've had a headache since I arrived in Blackheath. It comes and goes. I think it's just the beer and whisky, though I don't want to tell Mrs Moore that. I've been trying to hide my bags of bottles when I return to the house after going to the shops, and I get rid of the empties in a bin on the edge of the heath.

'Would you like some tablets?'

'No, I don't need any, thank you.'

'Stay where you are.' She walks slowly into her basement flat.

I've not been in her flat yet. She's never asked me in. I wait in the hallway, and while I wait I brush up the remaining ashes.

She returns after a few minutes, looks at the fireplace and then hands me a white plastic tub of tablets.

'Thank you.' I don't like the look she gives me. It's a knowing look. An expression of sympathy. She knows stuff. Or maybe it's just obvious that something has happened to me. Maybe I look like my life has just fallen apart, rather than just feeling it from the inside a little more every day.

'Goodbye, Mrs Moore.'

She smiles uneasily.

As I walk into the village I look at the tub to see how many tablets I might be able to take, but I see that they have gone out of date. They expired five years ago. I feel sorry for her when I see this. She must be confused to have kept something so many years past its expiry without realising it. I've not seen anyone visit or help her with anything. I put the tablets in the bin I use for my empty bottles.

I need to buy some clothes and I look in a couple of shops in the village, but as I have no income I decide I can't afford them and will make do with what I can find in the loft for now. Yesterday, I travelled a good few miles before withdrawing cash from our savings account. I don't want to use my debit card and let Mia know where I am. I also bought a cheap mobile phone. I still have the SIM card from the shattered pieces of phone which the girl with the pink jumper collected from the road and gave to me as I sat on the kerb after the crash. I've not switched on the new phone yet. I need to feel stronger before I can do that. More in control. I need a job.

I wander the aisles of a small supermarket a little aimlessly, some gravy granules the only thing in my basket. I can't think of what to buy. I look over the shelves at rows of oils, sauces, spices. We have a cupboard at home full of them, and as she cooked, Mia would pick them out so quickly that it seemed they were picked at random, though I'm sure they weren't. She'd pour and pinch and sprinkle and make everything taste perfect. Now, as I look at the jars and bottles along the shelves, I have no idea which ones we have at home and I don't even know the names of the ones I like. Mia would know.

At the butcher's counter, I ask for chicken breasts. Once they're bagged and in the basket, I move on to the vegetables and fill bags of carrots, swedes, broccoli, pick three red onions, a packet of tomatoes, mushrooms, courgettes. I go back to the aisle with the jars and bottles and pick up olive oil. Not the cheapest one, nor the most expensive. I recognise its label now.

At the freezers, I scan the shelves and tubs of ice cream. We've had mint and chocolate chip a lot lately. Maybe vanilla would make a nice change. I open the freezer door and reach for the tub, then change my mind last-minute and my hand drops to the next shelf and grabs a tub of raspberry ripple.

I walk out of the village and along the path that borders the heath towards my new home, with carrier bags dangling from my hands. There is a strong breeze now. Crows on the heath are struggling to land. I'm looking forward to getting back to the house. I feel excited at the thought of cooking a meal.

I walk up the stairs quickly, put the bags on the kitchen table and turn on the light. The day has passed quickly and it's getting dark already. I unpack the bags and switch the oven on. Its heat might warm the rooms or at least take the chill off them that comes with the darkness every night now.

The kitchen has everything I'll need, though it's all old stuff. I'm sure no one has lived in these rooms for a long while, and I wonder whose things these were, who's lived here before and who bought these things in the cupboards and drawers. I find baking pans in the storage under the oven and take two out. I put the chicken and potatoes in one, drizzle them with oil and put it in the oven. I turn back to the bags, take the ice cream out and put it in the freezer, the only item in there. Then I empty the bags and packets of vegetables onto the surface next to the sink. I wash them, wishing I had some music to put on. Listening to music while we cook always makes it more fun.

I chop and slice the vegetables, the sound of the knife tapping through the silence of the house, then I drop the pieces into the other pan. Slices of carrots, quarters of onions, cubes of courgette and batons of swede. They form a colourful mound. When I finish chopping and slicing, I flatten them out a little, pour on oil and put the pan in the oven. The table is littered with peels, ends, roots and little brown bits I've cut away. I gather them with the edge of my hand.

Water splashes loudly into the bath and steams gently around the bathroom. I wait until it's full before I undress, dropping my clothes on the floorboards around my feet. I feel the cold air and step into the water, a tingly burn against my quickly cooled skin. As I submerge myself to my chin, heat rushes over me and I gasp with relief.

I lie and watch the steam move around the room. The mirror above the sink has misted, and a patch, more lightly misted, shows where someone has wiped it before with their hand. I wonder when the last time was that someone laid in this bath. I rarely use the bath at home, always preferring the shower. Mia bathes every evening, pours powders and lotions under the taps into the splashing water. Scents of summer filled the house, even if it was winter. I lean forward and pick up the bottle of sports shower gel, the only toiletry I have, which I'd bought with the food shopping. I squeeze the bottle and a thick blue liquid stays just under the surface of the water between my knees. I wave my hand in the water and a small patch of white bubbles appear. I wave more, harder, but the bubbles don't grow anymore. I wash them around me and they spread in thin patches. I lie back and watch the steam.

My hand rests on my stomach. It's changed over the past few years and now has a slightly round feeling where there used to be a flat one, though I think it's got a little more flat again in the past couple of weeks. I look down between my legs. A useless body part now. My hand reaches down. Nothing feels the same anymore.

I rest in the warm water.

When my eyes open suddenly, I know that I've not been asleep. I smell the chicken and vegetables cooking and I feel stupid. It's the most like home that this house has felt since I arrived. I lean forward and pull the plug out, and as the water pours off me, I feel its coolness now.

I dry quickly and roughly with the brittle towel I found in the loft boxes, pick up my clothes from the floor and put them back on. The temperature has dropped despite the warm smell of cooking. I go to the kitchen, realising, feeling more awake by the second. I'm annoyed at myself.

I turn the oven off, pick up the oven gloves, take out the pans of half-cooked food and place them on the hob. Oil spits, and my earlier excitement of the meal has faded as quickly as the steam from the bath.

I've cooked for three. There's far too much meat and the vegetables don't look nice anymore. I don't know why I've bothered cooking at all. The chicken looks tasteless, the swedes unappetising. The onions are pointless.

I walk into the living room, stand at the window and look out over the darkness of the heath.

SIX

Great Aunt Ruth was more relaxed than my parents. She wore bright clothes, knitted herself scarves in pink and orange and yellow. Bright yellow, like a canary. She wore boots because she thought they looked good rather than for their practicality. Though she was in her eighties, she looked younger. Her hair was a perfect grey and shone like the inside of a sea shell. She wore jewellery, most of it worthless, except for a locket which her husband had given her. I would see it around her neck and wonder if it contained a tiny photo of them both. She smelled of lavender, wore the perfume on her neck and wrists and kept her clothes in drawers and wardrobes which hid little dry bags of it. She would know who was in the pop music charts, liked to watch a scary film. 'Be careful you don't get yourself into trouble, run up debts or get anyone pregnant,' she said to me once. Mum was horrified. Dad just rolled his eyes. I was only ten. I don't know what she thought I was getting up to in my free time.

I'd seen photos of her from when she was young and she looked rigid, more reserved in her style and even in her expression. Mum and Dad said her extravagant nature was due to her getting old and going a bit funny, but I always thought it was something else. I thought her to be, due to her old age, more experienced than the rest of us and therefore knew better, like her understanding of life had taught her to express herself and be whoever she wanted to be. I thought she was the coolest person in the world.

She lived on her own in a small house in Brighton. Mum and Dad and I visited her there sometimes. She did a lot of things for the community and for the church, even though she wasn't religious. She was always busy, her diary always full. I thought it was her mind which kept her face young. It simply didn't have time to get too old. She worked part-time in a charity shop and had a good friend, an ex-army guy who was about the same age and lived a few houses away from her. They would drink port together in the evenings and listen to old records on the turntable in her living room.

Aunt Ruth was convinced that our house in Whiteflower Woods was haunted. She'd light candles and Mum would go around blowing them out, saying she was mad. Aunt Ruth would look at me and shake her head. 'I think someone's watching over you, Lewis,' she said quietly to me one day as we sat in the garden, like she was revealing a secret. Mum overheard and was furious, and even Dad was that time. I felt on edge after, thinking that I was being watched. I had to sleep with the light on for weeks and weeks, held a bath towel around me as I got undressed, even though I would be the only person I could see in the room. Carl slept on my bedroom floor to keep me company.

Carl lived with his parents and his sister Kelly, who was a few years older than us. His dad was tough. I never understood how his mum and dad had formed a life together as she was so quiet, so polite. She fussed over Carl and Kelly, did everything she could to make them happy. She put her life into her house and family, worked part-time as a dinner lady, and all the money she earned bought things for those two.

His dad spent much of his spare time in The Pheasant, watching the TV there after going into town to put bets on. When he had a good win they'd be treated, but when he hadn't, or if he was too drunk, the three of them, and even me, knew to stay out of his way. He gave Carl a hard time, often in front of me or others, and would tell him he was a wimp, which he wasn't, and would give him a shove on the shoulder or chest as he said it. I'm sure he would have been pleased if Carl had laid into him with fists flying and legs kicking, though he would definitely have come off worse. I could always see, though, that it wasn't physical strength or lack of temper that made Carl not fight back. It was something his dad couldn't see. Carl was clever. He knew that not reacting would piss his dad off more than anything.

Kelly thought we were disgusting. We thought she was stuck-up, always thinking that she was grown up and that we were just kids. She'd have guys in cars come to pick her up for nights out in The Pheasant and we'd tease her for her make-up, tell her she looked like a clown, even when she looked nice. She'd dress immaculately for going out, but would wear shorts and jumpers to dig vegetables from the garden with her mum too. She spent lots of time in her bedroom writing stories, and we'd call her a geek. She would tell on us for anything she caught us doing and sometimes for things we hadn't even done. We once found a toad in the woods and put it in her bedroom when she was out, then when she got home we sat in the garden laughing, waiting to hear her scream.

Mum worked with Carl's mum as a dinner lady too. They were good friends and each was the only friend the other had really. When we were at first school, they'd be waiting together at the school gates to walk us home. We were always so pleased to see them.

Dad rarely yelled, was never violent towards me, but he had a different way of being authoritative, controlling even.

Disappointment. I never felt good enough. I struggled to remember things. He or Mum would ask me to go the shop in the village to get something, put the money in my hand and I'd walk straight there. When I got there I might not remember what it was I needed to buy. I'd have to walk back home and ask them again what it was and say that I didn't mind walking back to the village. Dad wouldn't let Mum write things down for me. He said he was trying to help, but the only person who really helped me was Carl. I'd go next door and ask him if he wanted to walk to the village with me, so he'd remember what it was. I knew we'd be friends forever, because I wouldn't know what to do without him.

SEVEN

It's late morning. I stand in the entrance to *Michael's*. It's a nice-looking, small restaurant on the edge of the heath, glass-walled with a tiny bar in the corner. It's bright and lively. Most of the tables have diners at them. A postcard in the window said help was needed, though it didn't say what for. Maybe I should pin a similar sign to myself. A grey, slightly balding man walks towards me. He looks in a hurry.

'Table for one?'

'I wanted to ask about the vacancy advertised in the window.' My voice sounds dry. I've not spoken to anyone for days. 'My name's Lewis.'

'I'm Michael, nice to meet you.' His handshake is gentle. 'Have you done waitering before?'

He looks at me attentively now. He has a good smile and one pearl earring. He is quite old, but definitely not frail. I think he's probably older than he looks too. He's well presented, but not posh-looking. I can imagine him as a younger man, jetting around the world to attend extravagant parties or something.

'To be honest, I've never been a waiter.'

'What's your previous experience?'

'In administration,' I say, realising I'm doing a terrible job at selling myself.

'So why are you asking me for a job?' he asks in a genuine, interested kind of way, like there must be a good reason, but that he needs some help grasping it.

'I've just moved to the area. I live just up the road,' I say, trying to sell at least one good point of employing me, that I'm local.

'Can you start right now?'

I hesitate. I'd not really thought about getting a job much, until I saw the postcard in the window.

'Yes.'

'Great, you can do the lunch rush with me. Eugene has called in sick and left me in it. I'd guess he was out last night and hasn't made it home yet,' he says, as if it's happened before. 'Jessica!' He calls to a waitress who has just rushed past us with a plate of sandwiches in each hand. 'This is Lewis. He's having a test run this afternoon to see if he likes the place.'

I like the way he describes it as me checking them out rather than the other way around, but I feel I need to say something. I need to tell him that really I'm not ready for this, that I haven't prepared myself for it, but I realise now that I can't say anything.

'Hi, Lewis.'

Jessica's light brown hair is straight and just about rests on her shoulder on one side and is pulled back on the other side by a clip with a plastic yellow flower on it. She's pretty, has a fresh-looking face and wide-open eyes. They're concentrated on me, thinking something, though I don't know what. Normally this would make me feel uneasy, but I feel comfortable in front of her.

'Hi, Jessica.'

Michael takes me into a large kitchen. It's very clean but everything is old.

'It'll have to be a quick tour as we do get busy around this time. I make most of the food in the afternoons. We only open at eleven, so no breakfasts, then the chef comes in at six for dinner reservations. The lunch menu is sandwiches and toasties and things like that. Anything cooked properly is on the evening menu and left to the chef who has much better cooking skills than me.'

Jessica bangs through the swing doors into the kitchen, tears a page from her notepad and attaches it to the fridge door with a magnet. She picks up a plate of sandwiches and bangs back through the doors and is gone.

'Follow her, do what she does.'

I go out into the restaurant and feel my heart pounding. Once Jessica has taken the plate to one of the tables, she walks back, takes a notepad and pen from her apron pocket and hands it to me. For a moment I don't know what to do, where to look or what to say, and I feel a sudden, light sweat over my face. Jessica has walked off again and speaks to a couple who just come in the door, then shows them to a table. I look around. A woman at the far end of the restaurant has her hand in the air. After a few seconds I realise she's waving at me and I slowly walk towards her, having no idea what I'm going to do when I reach her.

I leave my first shift at *Michael's* and begin to walk across the heath.

I've spent the past few hours doing something, which is something I've hardly done in recent weeks. I've had small conversations with people, taken their orders and written them down on my notepad. When I took my first order I panicked, as I couldn't think how to write and for a moment my pen just stood still on the paper, until it began to move across the little page. I'd forgotten what my handwriting looks like. I took plates of food from the kitchen to tables, learned how to operate a coffee machine and a till, opened cans of fizzy drinks and poured them into glasses filled with ice. I've been told I have a job to go back to tomorrow. I feel like I should be proud of myself. I'm not, but I feel now that there is a purpose for tomorrow happening.

I walk across the heath and notice the feeling of distractedness, which I've had for weeks, begin to return. I've been functioning today, somehow doing things, though I don't know how. Even though it was only taking people's lunch orders and the odd short conversation with Jessica and Michael, it made me feel more alive than I've felt since before the morning of the crash. Today, it felt like I had something to do, a reason for being. Now, I feel it draining from me, as the realisation of my situation returns, and I frown. I'm sure this persistent frown is one of the reasons for my headaches, which I'm having nearly every day now. I wish Aunt Ruth was still alive, so I could call her and tell her about all this. She'd know what to do. I try to push the deep lines out of my forehead with my fingertips. I've never known a feeling like this. I think it's grief.

I sit on the bench next to the pond as my legs have begun to shake. I think of Mia and Carl. The sobbing sound she made after they'd seen me, as he lay on my side of the bed with his hands cupped between his legs. Such a silly image, it feels like I couldn't have seen it at all. I feel as haunted as the oldest house, and I'm sure it's a feeling that's never, ever going to go away.

It'll begin to get dark soon. I can see the first signs of it in the sky, but I'm not ready to walk back to the house yet. I just need a moment. As I look out over the grass, the pond and the trees, I appreciate the peace that comes with the space here. When I sit on the heath, it feels like the world stops with me.

There's something I need to do and I don't want to do it in the house as I want to try to leave the thought of it out here on the heath, so that I might have a better chance of sleep tonight.

I take my new mobile phone from my pocket and then

look for my old SIM card, which I'd been keeping in my wallet. As I take it out, I try not to glimpse at the photo of me and Mia. I'm not sure I can keep the photo with me any longer, though I don't feel I can take it out of my wallet either. I put the SIM card in place and switch the phone on. My hands are shaking. After a few seconds there is a chorus of bleeps and flashes as messages come through.

Are you OK? Where are you? I'm so worried.

Lewis, I'm so sorry.

They found your car crashed, please call me, please, please call me.

Lewis, please call me.

Lewis, I can explain.

They go on and on.

Hi, I'm OK. Sorry not been in touch before, will be again soon. Lewis.

I send both of them the same text. Within seconds my phone starts ringing and *Mia* appears on the lit screen. The thought of speaking to her fills me with dread, because I know I have nothing to say to her and that confuses me more than anything I've ever known. How can I have nothing to say to her? Maybe it's what she has to say to me that worries me more. I switch the phone off and put it into my pocket.

A guy sits down next to me. I glance sideways at his face. He looks at his hands, which rest together on his lap.

A heron stands in the pond. It's a skinny bird, dolphin-coloured with yellow stick legs. It stares downwards, very still. Fishing. The water looks brown and dark from here but I know it's actually clear and shallow and full of gudgeon, as I've looked into it on my many walks here over the past few weeks. Around the edges are thick, wide green reeds, and a patch of lilies lie near the middle. Now, as October ends, the duckweed from summer has nearly all gone. I can smell the earthy water. Above the little trees on the far side of the pond I see the church steeple pointing into the sky and behind that an orange and yellow kite. It gets lower and lower and then drops from the sky.

I think this is my favourite part of the heath. It's incredibly soothing, and though I hear traffic from the main road, gently buzzing, a breeze steadily brushing by my ears and an occasional laugh or shout from the pub someway behind me, everything feels at a distance. There's only me, the heron and the guy, and none of us makes a sound. We've spent a little while in each other's company but in our own worlds, though I wish he hadn't sat on the bench with me. It feels like my respite is being a little intruded upon.

I glance at the guy's leg. He's wearing bleached blue jeans. His black boots, their laces undone, sit crossed on top of one another. He sighs, and I look back at the heron, who watches us for a few seconds as if he'd heard the sigh, then looks back down at the water. I look at the sky and the kite that has just soared again from behind the church. It's such a beautiful place, Blackheath. Even though my reason for being here is so unimaginably awful that I don't think it has even begun to sink in yet, I can't help but notice its beauty. It's a place that I could, and might, stay for good. Though it isn't home.

Home is where Mia is.

And Carl.

I look over to my new home. It's a fair distance away from the pond, over the grass and a couple of roads. I think of Mrs Moore in the basement flat. The house is just a minute or two walk from the village, and though it has another house close to either side of it, it looks remote. From another time or place. Like the only house on that road which has no one living in it.

I suddenly become aware, and I don't even need to turn to make sure, that the guy is looking at me now. Looking at my face, which is just inches away from his. My heart races. My mouth has gone dry. I'm not sure if he's going to speak to me, or mug me, or what, but I have an overwhelming feeling that something isn't right. I want to get up and walk away and am about to do so when he stands. He takes a few steps then stops, turns back and looks at me. He holds a cigarette between his fingers.

'Have you got a light?'

He's younger than me, much younger. Maybe still a teenager. His eyes are as green as grass and are looking into me, waiting for an answer. His hair is dark and shaved short. Two gold hoop earrings hang shining from his left ear. His white T-shirt is too small for him and the black leather jacket, which he pulls on after resting the cigarette in his lips, is too big. It hangs off him. There is something in his expression. I find him intimidating.

'I've not, I'm sorry.'

'Don't be sorry, mate.' He smiles and winks and walks away, and his dog, a little reddish terrier which I'd not noticed until now, follows. His walk is a confident, laddish walk with fluid footsteps that fall wide apart from one another. I don't walk like him. His walk looks uncomfortable but somehow instinctive. Natural. I watch, until he and his dog are very tiny figures, going over the heath and out of sight.

I take my mobile from my pocket and switch it on again. More bleeps of messages. I read them. Messages of worry, of concern, of begging me to get in touch. Some from Mia and some from Carl. I listen to twelve voicemails from them too. In some messages her voice is pure panic, asking for forgiveness. In others she is yelling and demanding that I call, saying she can't cope with this anymore. Carl is calm, asking for us to meet, saying he can explain. There are a couple of messages where there is near silence. Someone wanting to speak but unable to find the words. I know this is Carl. I can't listen to all of the messages, and I begin to delete them as soon as they begin.

I sit up straight, as if I need to be professional for a moment, to stop myself from falling apart. I must keep it together.

I stare at the skinny heron and he stares at the pond.

EIGHT

I can't remember anyone actually telling me that I had two dads, one that was alive and who wrote his letters in his office in the spare room and mowed the weed-free lawn, and another who was in heaven, but my knowledge of this grew up with me.

It had David Brown named as my father on my birth certificate, but I knew this to be a massive fib. My real dad died in a plane crash, leaving Mum broken-hearted. She had to hide her heartbreak, as she'd married my other dad a year earlier. It was back when Mum had lived in London. How she had started an affair I could never, even in my adult life, understand, and I could never ask. There was an unspoken ban on the whole subject, though I remember feeling brave and asking her once, when I was about twelve, what my dad's name was, and she said the name that's on my birth certificate, without even flinching. I knew then that there was so much more than a name that she wasn't telling me, and I knew I could never ask again. I loved Mum and didn't want to upset her.

The plane crash also turned out to be a fib, though of

my own making. I knew he had died in some kind of accident. At first I imagined it to be a train crash, then a bus and finally, I decided, a plane crash must have been it. I told Aunt Ruth this one day, as fact, while we sat in her garden.

'No he didn't. He slipped on the snow and banged his head, on his way to work.'

I was shocked. I'd never heard of someone dying because of falling over, and I was overcome, thinking what a terrible thing it was for him to die in the morning, when everything is just beginning again.

'Are you sure that's how it happened?'

She thought for a moment, but I knew she was just pretending to have a think, so I'd know her answer was right.

'Yes. Absolutely.' She nodded a couple of times as she said it and held the ties of her headscarf under her chin. She'd been wearing it a lot that summer, as it annoyed Mum. 'On his way to work one morning.'

'Did you know him?'

'Yes, of course. We got on like a house on fire.'

Two winters later – it was that long before there was sufficient snowfall in Whiteflower – I tried again and again to slip in the snow, but it was impossible. Ice I could slip on, but not snow. It must have been ice, I told Aunt Ruth, but she just shook her head and said nothing. I knew then that Mum had told her off for talking to me about him.

At school, I struggled. Carl and I were in the same classes for games, religious education and were in the same registration class. For other subjects, Carl was ahead of me and was in the highest set for maths, English literature, science and geography, when I was in the second-lowest. He was in the classes with the people who, by the age of thirteen, had already decided which universities they were going to apply for. Carl stood out from them. They were too well mannered to make him feel completely excluded, but they didn't like him. He didn't like them either, but even though his home life was so different to those clever people around him, he had manners good enough to show them up, so they never knew.

Carl's parents had more money than mine. I don't know how; I guess his dad got paid more than mine, even though they worked in similar trades. They had a nicer garden. Carl's mum would buy extra sweets and biscuits when she went shopping so there was enough for me at their house too. It's not that I wasn't provided for by my parents, but that was all they could afford to do. Ice pops and sweets and really thick chocolate spread on toast I got at Carl's house. They had a car, too, whereas we didn't. Carl's dad would devote hours each week to maintaining its engine and shining its exterior. He tried to teach Carl about the engine but he didn't have much interest in it, though he would never have told his dad that and neither would I. Carl learned about spark plugs and batteries, brake fluids and oils, tyres and air. At the end of these summer days the two of them would be covered – hands, arms and streaky faces – with black grease. His dad would wash his hands and leave the rest. Carl would scrub and scrub to get rid of the grease and his dad would tell him he was acting like a girl, which would make him scrub harder.

There were no grandparents left in my family, but Carl's grandparents, on his dad's side, were still alive when we were young. They'd been together since they were teenagers, had kids early on, four of them, Carl's dad being the eldest. Carl's grandad was a much more gentle man and he worked hard all his life while his wife raised their children. They both had such pride in telling me and Carl stories from their lives before either of us had been born. They seemed ancient to us. They were still in love in their old age, and it was obvious to see. Their happiness, smiles and laughs were infectious. Me and Carl would ride our bikes to visit them. It was a long ride through the Sussex woods and fields to their little house with the big garden.

We hadn't yet had girlfriends, but some of our friends were beginning to have brief and intense romances. Carl talked a lot about girls and said he'd definitely have a girlfriend one day. I wasn't sure if I would or not. We didn't know much on the subject, but we knew that the most passionate thing you could do with a girl was French kissing, only we didn't really know what it was.

When we were twelve, his grandad passed away after a very short illness. The whole family were with him when he passed and they were all devastated. I went to the funeral, the first one Carl and I had been to, and we stood side by side at the grave in the first suits we'd ever worn. Nothing prepared us for the rawness of a funeral. Nothing made us leave each other's side that day.

We continued our bike rides and visits to his nan, but she was never the same. She became quiet. She was always pleased to see us, but I never saw her laugh again. Smiles, but never laughs.

When we arrived at her house she would always be sitting at the little garden table under the pear tree if it was warm, or if it was cold or raining she would be sitting in the porch chair and looking out of the window into the front garden. I always wondered what she thought about in those quiet times by herself.

NINE

I stand in front of the window in the living room. I've become a daydreamer since I've been on my own and especially in the early mornings when I look out of the windows. It's a great view over the heath from here. There is so much to see.

Joggers are out already, going along the little maze-like pathways across the grass. Some people just wander around. Someone sits on the bench on the edge of the heath opposite, their back to the house. A pigeon lands on the window ledge and I take a slow step back so as not to scare him. He watches me with a look of expectation, as behind him the hopeful glow of sunrise emerges over the heath. So much life from one window. So little life going on inside it.

I look out at the early view most mornings now. I don't really sleep for a full night anymore and I can't deal with my empty bed. I never used to mind this before. If Mia were to get up early for some reason, I'd stretch out, but now the emptiness is unbearable. When I wake up, which is usually when it's still dark, I get out of bed because I know that sleep isn't going to come again. Then I stand and watch this view of the sun rising.

This house is not a home. It still doesn't look like anyone lives here. There is only one item of furniture in the living room, the sofa, which was covered with a sheet when I arrived. It's placed diagonally, facing the fireplace with the boards nailed across it. I sit on the sofa and look around the room. My room. My new living room, which has no life in it at all. No voices, no TV, no music.

No Mia and no Carl.

I need to ask Mrs Moore if I can take the boards off and whether the chimney will be clean enough to light a fire. It's too cold. The fireplaces are lit in the bedroom and empty room. I try to keep them going as Mrs Moore asked, to stop damp taking hold of the house.

Mia would like the fireplace in the bathroom. I think of her when I bathe. I light the fire just before I get in the bath and lie there in the steamy, flickering light. I lie and think until the water and the memories turn cold.

In Blackheath I feel a long way from her, and in some way I am. I think it might take an hour by car if not travelling in rush hour. Close, but far away. I'd do anything to have her near me, to put my arm around her here on the sofa, lie against her in bed, but I know I can't. I know I can't ever again. There's no going back. Mia has no going back. Nor Carl either. It's broken.

I sit in my empty living room, looking around where there is nothing to look at. No one to speak to. I've never felt alone before. The home that Mia and I made, and which Carl was a big part of, was a warm, happy place. We would watch films in the evenings, drink beer and wine and eat food that Mia would make for us and put on plates on the glass coffee table. Mia and I would lie on the sofa and Carl would sit in his armchair next to the TV. There was both nothing and everything in those evenings at home together. I always felt grateful for my relationships with both of them. I knew how rare they were. Carl would stay in his own flat a few nights a week, but he stayed in our box room as and when he wanted to. He didn't even need to ask. It was his room.

I wonder if Mia ever went to his flat without me. I wonder if she went to him in the box room when he was at home and I wasn't. I wonder if they shared meals at his flat and if he ever made love to her on his living room floor. If he ever made love to her on my living room floor.

I rub my forehead, my eyes. They both ache so much.

I wonder if Mia is at home and whether Carl is there. I want to know what she did today, feel the need to be her listener. A good listener is one of the most treasurable things to find. Aunt Ruth told me that. Mia, Carl and I always listened to one another. No problem or subject was too personal, no thoughts or worries too silly. We just talked and talked.

I wonder if she's lying amongst the white sheets of our bed, her long dark hair strewn on the pillows, shining from the first line of daylight between the gap in the curtains, like I used to see when I woke before her. I wonder if Carl is there too. Maybe they're both alone, as I am. I hate the things that I don't know. They hurt me more than the things I do know. I'm sure of it.

Bastards.

I walk around the house, along the hallways, looking in the doorways. I only looked around on the first day I arrived, and when I did so then there were only bare and empty rooms, without even any carpets. With Mrs Moore in the basement flat, me in the top floor, the middle area of the house – the first and ground floors – feel somewhat abandoned. I remember her telling me that she used to run it as a boarding house and wonder now why she doesn't still do so. These hallways and rooms must have been teeming with life.

On the first floor, just at the top of the stairs, by the large window that looks out over the heath, I find a door which is closed. White and wooden, with a round brass handle and a keyhole, the same as all the other doors in the house. The closed door wakes my curiosity. The only other doors that I've seen closed are those belonging to cupboards, the tiny staircase to the loft and the door to the basement flat. I hear a grandfather clock chime five times. I've not seen it but I've heard it ticking before. It's the first time I've noticed its chime.

A closed door makes me want to open it.

I don't feel like I'm snooping, though I suppose I am a little. It's Mrs Moore's house, but it feels like she just lives in the basement. The two middle floors are a no-man's land. This house must be so very old.

Hearing no movement from inside the door, I turn its handle. It rattles in my grip. I don't remember any rooms being locked when I had my look around on the day I moved in. I look along the landing and see the other rooms with their doors slightly open. Emerging daylight pours from them. Maybe Mrs Moore has some belongings locked away in this room. I kneel, put my eye to the keyhole. My heart races as I know I shouldn't be doing this, but there's nothing but darkness in the room.

I try the handle once more.

Definitely locked.

TEN

Winters in Whiteflower were perfectly endless. Snow would drift up to the windowsills. Icicles hung from trees like frozen fruits. Frosts would lie like a thick, crunchy carpet. As a lot of children came from other villages to attend our school and would be unable to do so on the snow-covered roads, which no one ever came to salt as they were too remote, school often closed for a few days at a time. Carl and I would spend these days building snowmen and little igloos and then have the evenings in front of the fireplace in his living room or mine, drinking hot chocolate with our feet stretched out and warming in front of the flames through thick socks.

As much as the winters were fun, the spring and summers were heaven.

Most of our time was spent outside. Our garden was basic. A lawn, which Dad always kept as short and weed-free as he could manage. Pansies grew in the borders.

Carl's garden was just as important to his family as the inside of their house. They grew vegetables, rows and rows of potatoes, carrots, cabbages, lettuces, radishes and turnips.

Tomatoes and runner beans grew between and were supported by lengths of green string, their fruits dangling until they ripened in the late summer sun. Apple, pear and plum trees grew at the end of the garden. Carl's mum spent hours maintaining, pruning, watering and harvesting. She passed bowls of fruit and vegetables over the fence to Mum and made pies for other people in the village. Every meal they had would have a salad beside it during the summer months. They had a lawn too, nicely kept but full of dandelions – they didn't mind them – and in the beds that weren't working hard growing vegetables, forget-me-nots scattered blue in the spring and roses bloomed in every colour as the year wore on.

Whiteflower Woods surrounded our houses. Carl and I explored them continuously. In spring, we'd collect frogspawn in buckets from the streams and pools of water in the ditches and bring it back to the pond in Carl's garden, until it looked like the pond would overflow with it. When it began to hatch, the pond became a squirming black mass of tadpoles, which we fed on fruit and vegetable peel. We'd run down the garden waving our arms and yelling when we caught his cat trying to scoop them out. As the tadpoles grew legs, our parents and Carl's sister Kelly would go mad as hundreds of black frogs, the size of a little fingernail, jumped around the garden, making the lawn look like a giant green head of hair with lice leaping from it, before they set off into the woods.

Trees kept us occupied for hours. We had rope swings. Pieces of timber, which Carl's dad would cut for us, made little seats amongst the branches. We were constantly finding new challenges about the height we would climb to, and would dare each other to go higher. There were crab apple trees, hundreds of them, covered in blossom in spring and then filled with little fruits and little birds that pecked at them in the autumn. Horse chestnut trees grew prize conkers, which we'd search the ground for and Carl's dad would drill for us to put string through. Oaks everywhere. The woods were full of everything.

We spent nearly all of our time together, Carl and I. We'd walk to school together, walk home together through the country roads when we got too old for our mums to be waiting at the school gates. We'd spend evenings at each other's houses, or be out playing football or riding our bikes, which we did everywhere, going much longer distances than our parents ever knew about. We wanted to explore.

Lost in innocence, the years were long. It felt like we'd always be young. I never imagined those days ending.

ELEVEN

It's been cool for a couple of weeks. There's more darkness than light. Today, though, there seems to be a little reprieve. The sky is clear, blue as a jay's wing. I can feel the sun's warmth through my clothes and there's only a gentle breeze. I think, as I walk home from work, that I'll sit on the heath for a while before I go back to the house. It might be the last day I can sit outside comfortably until spring.

On a bench not far from the house, I sit and stretch my legs full and straight. I have a polystyrene cup of tea which I made myself just before I left the restaurant. I take a few sips as I look across the heath. A mass of dark grey clouds pass over Canary Wharf. I can see the tops of the tallest buildings there. They're full of lights. As the clouds cover them and the view becomes hazy, I guess from rain, it looks like the building tops are in a little patch of night.

Someone sits next to me and I glance at him, then back at the storm. It's the guy who sat next to me on the bench beside the pond. I've seen him a few times since, walking the heath with his little reddish dog now sitting beside his boots. All three of us watch the gathering clouds.

'The storm is growing.'

I don't like a stranger talking to me. He looks at me with a slight smile, a smirk, even. He's picked up on my discomfort and obviously finds it funny.

'My name's Parker.'

He holds out his hand to shake mine. I think for a moment about making a name up, but then, without meaning to, I'm speaking to him.

'I'm Lewis.'

He seems pleased that I've let my guard down and shakes my hand roughly in two strokes. There is something old-fashioned in his mannerisms, a gentlemanly quality about him, yet he still looks like he could rob me. His confidence makes me nervous.

We look back at the storm. It's moving fast and must be crossing the river at Greenwich by now. A strong, cool breeze rushes over my face. It's almost cold again, the unexpected good weather blowing away.

'How long do you reckon we got?' Parker doesn't take his eyes off the storm as he speaks, and his smirk has appeared again, like he's enjoying watching it.

'A few minutes I'd say.'

'At the most.'

A streak of lightning flashes down and touches Greenwich Park. It's close now. A grumble of thunder follows, so loud and deep that it shakes the bench. The little dog jumps onto Parker's lap. He puts his arm around him and strokes the top of his head with the back of his finger a few times. I look at the dog, who looks back at me warily. It's like the one I saw on the opposite side of the road as I sat on the kerb after crashing my car.

The dog looks back at the storm. A moody darkness has fallen over the heath, but it's not real. A fake dusk. Ash-grey clouds come over us and I hear the first signs of rain. The breeze returns and this time blows persistently, like a fan.

'Right, I'm running for it.' I stand up from the bench,

drop my cup of tea into the bin and turn to Parker. 'Are you?'

'No.' He looks from the storm to me, with his deep green eyes.

There's no immediate shelter. The bandstand would take five minutes to reach.

'I live just over there.' I point to the house. 'Come inside until the storm passes.'

'Are you sure?'

His dog reluctantly jumps to the ground as Parker stands.

'Absolutely.'

We begin to walk, and then we run towards the house as rain starts to fall suddenly and loudly. Rain everywhere, drenching rain. It hits the ground and splatters back up, a frenzy of splashes, flying in all directions. The air is thick with it. My hair is soaked in seconds and sticks to my forehead. Streams run down my face and into my eyes. I wipe them out with my fingertips and new streams flow into them.

We reach the house in less than a minute and I open the door. Parker takes his boots off just inside and I slip my trainers off too.

'Shit, why did we leave it so late before we ran?' Parker asks with a laugh as he follows me up the stairs.

'I was just thinking the same thing.' I realise I'm smiling, almost laughing. I think it might be the first time I've done so in weeks. My cheeks feel tight from the smile.

I walk into the living room, the almost empty living room. I've still bought hardly anything. I don't even have a towel to offer Parker to dry himself on, only the brittle one I found in the loft, and I'd be too embarrassed to offer that to a guest. I feel ashamed at what he must think of my home.

'Those flowers smell nice.' He takes a deep breath. Even his little dog raises his head and sniffs the air, his eyes squinting.

'There are no flowers up here. That smell has been here since I moved in a few weeks ago. I don't know where it's coming from.'

We look at one another, our faces dripping with rain. He looks as if he's expecting me to say something else, but I don't know what to say so I walk to the window. He follows and then stands beside me.

The heath has disappeared behind a sheet of grey-white, as if we're standing in a shelter under a waterfall. The sound of the pelting against the walls and windows is as loud as a running bath. The storm is overwhelming, a giant. We watch and listen. Parker picks up his little dog and he watches too. Everything stops. There's an intense feeling of peace, as restful as sleep.

'Thanks,' Parker says. He looks at me.

The intimidation I felt earlier has gone.

'Can I get you a drink of anything?'

'Are you sure?'

'Yeah. Tea? Beer?'

'Tea, thanks.'

I stand at the sink and fill the kettle, unsure now if I've been stupid by letting a stranger into the house. I wonder what he's doing in the other room while I am out of sight in the kitchen and I try to hurry as I put teabags and milk into cups.

'Sugar?' I call.

'Two please.' His voice is quiet. He's standing behind me. I spin around and I think he sees my suddenness.

'If that's OK?' he says, as if I was shocked by his reply.

'Of course.'

The kettle begins to purr, and a little steam wafts from its spout.

'Do you live locally?' I ask, thinking I already know the answer.

'Sort of.'

'And work?'

'I don't work anymore, but I used to be a park-keeper. That's how I got my nickname.'

I'd not even thought about Parker not being his real name. It fits him so naturally. I want to ask his real name now, but as he's told me Parker, I guess that's what he likes to be called.

'You're always walking on the heath.' I meant to think it, but I said it out loud.

'I like to give Stamp a good run about.' Stamp looks up when he hears his name. Parker squats beside him and strokes his head a few times. 'I've seen you about quite a bit too, but only recently. I guess you've just moved here?'

'Yeah.' I can't remember how many weeks it's been now. Three. Maybe four.

The kettle clicks off and I pour steaming water into cups. It's the first time in a while I've made more than one cup of tea. I'm used to making them in twos or threes at home. I feel a sense of hope from seeing two cups, stirring one, then the other.

I pass Parker his tea, pick up mine and then walk into the living room.

The rain has slowed, but only a little. It's still the heaviest rain I've ever seen. Lightning flashes and thunder crashes. I used to enjoy watching a thunderstorm. I used to enjoy a lot of things.

'So where did you live before?' Parker takes little sips. It must be far too hot.

'Putney, but I grew up in Sussex.'

'Nice area, Putney. How come you moved?'

'I've left my wife.'

The enormity of the words, spoken out loud for the first time, take the air out of me, like I've just knocked something very strong back in one go.

'Oh, right.' Parker looks a little sorry he asked.

I realise we are looking at each other and I look back out of the window at the storm.

I've left my wife.

I watch the rain and the flashes and feel like the most selfish person in the world.

TWELVE

As we became teenagers, we still fished the lake in the woods. We caught, at different times of the year, the little fleeting roach, fat carp and burly brown tench. Perch, striped and colourful, like a clown's face, and pike with sharp white teeth, like cat fangs. The golden tench still eluded us. Carl's nan, who fished when she was young, one day told us of a technique she'd heard her father speak of but which they'd never tried. The technique was to rake the bottom of an area of lake bed. This would make the water muddy and cloudy, stir up food to attract fish and, most importantly, might lure tench, who are thought to be an inquisitive species, to come and investigate the disturbance.

One summer day, she took us out to the shed in her garden, which still contained all of Carl's grandad's tools, years after he had passed. Standing in the doorway of the shed and seeing them inside, it felt, just for a moment, that he was alive again. I looked at Carl and he gave me a glance, which told me he was thinking the same thing, and he sighed. We didn't always speak in words.

She took the head off a rake. It was a heavy, solid, five-pronged rake, like some kind of medieval torture instrument. She also found some thin rope, which she told us Carl's grandad had once tried to make her a washing line with.

The following day, straight after school, Carl and I went to our usual fishing spot, where, from a young age, and still then on occasions, we'd hug the low, overhanging branches and watch the fish when we were bored.

We unravelled the rope, tied the rake head onto it and began to take it in turns to throw it out into the water as far as we could, while the other held the end of the rope and pulled it back over the lake bed. It splashed over and over again. Carl could throw further than me. The swans, who usually stayed close to us, swam away and congregated on the little island in the middle of the lake, as if to discuss what the hell we were playing at.

We had cast the rake out in the shape of a fan, covering as much area as we could, and my arms hurt, veins ached and muscles felt bruised.

'My arms really fucking ache now.'

'Mine too, they're fucked!'

We'd only started to use the F-word that summer, but were managing to fit it into almost every sentence out of earshot of our parents.

We stood at the water's edge, rubbing our upper arms as if it was freezing cold, but late-afternoon sun was shining warmly across the lake and it drenched us with its light. Carl's nan had told us we should wait an hour or so after the raking, so we lay on our backs in the long grass and, as we had done so many times over so many years before, we dozed as crickets sung and hopped around us.

Carl cast first. We made a plan that we would each cast for ten minutes to make it fair, though neither of us seemed very hopeful of the golden tench. We'd tried so many times before. The surface of the water was perfectly flat and still and showed none of the signs of feeding fish that we knew to look for. As always, we used no floats or other bite indicators, just a line with a weight on it to help with distance and a small hook on the end with a pierced grain of sweetcorn.

Carl's cast landed with a subtle plop, which seemed stealthy in comparison to the crashing through the water of the rake head an hour before, and I realised as the ripples began to settle that the swans hadn't returned. I looked across the lake and saw them still standing on the little island, watching us.

Carl stood with the line in his fingertips and I sat cross-legged beside him, and we both looked out into the silence. I don't think we spoke to each other once while we waited. Carl is the only person with whom I've ever been able to have comfortable silences. Over the years before that day, during our childhood, and in the years after, there were hundreds of these comfortable moments. Neither of us looked at our watches to check when his ten minutes would be over, and I have no idea how long we were staring at the lake, lost in our thoughts, but all of a sudden there was a swirling swell and then a splash of water.

The second it was hooked, the fish headed straight out into the depths. The rod bent and the reel screeched as line was pulled from it at speed. Then the fish stopped. It was a while before it responded to gentle tugs on the line, but in stops and starts, it began to come towards us. The fight lasted much longer than usual. The small fish we could land in seconds, the larger ones in a few minutes, and even the fattest carp in the lake we had landed in less than fifteen, but Carl said he was taking his time to make sure the fish was exhausted first. More than ever, we didn't want it to get away. I scrambled up a branch to look into the water to see the species and size, but to my surprise the water was still cloudy, almost opaque in the fading light. The sun was just beginning to set.

As the battle neared its end, I took my trainers and socks

off and paddled a few feet out into the water, ready to get hold of the fish, to reduce the chances of its escape as soon as it lifted its head above the surface and gave up its fight.

Eventually, the fish poked its golden head out of the water and lay on its side as Carl pulled it in the last little distance. I grabbed one hand around its gills and the other around the base of its tail and carried it to the bank, where Carl was *woohoo*-ing.

'You fucking did it,' I said.

'*We* fucking did it.'

One of the golden tench we'd been trying to catch for years now lay on the grass in front of us. We knelt either side of it as I slipped the hook gently from its lip. It was a sturdy-looking fish, muscular, and weighed around two pounds, we guessed after both holding it. Definitely not a monster. Enough to feed two, maybe. I put my fingers in my mouth and then ran them down the fish's side. It felt like wet leather.

After we'd had a good look, we both picked it up. Four hands covered nearly all of its golden skin and scales and we held it upright in the shallows until it got its watery breath back and swam slowly away. We scrambled up the low branches to see if we could watch it some more, but there was just dark water and then the swans coming back across the lake towards us.

THIRTEEN

In the afternoon lull, where Michael has said he can manage on his own, Jessica and I are sitting at a table in the corner of the restaurant having our break with some food we made for ourselves.

'Do you live locally?' I ask.

'Yeah, just up the road. I'm housemates with Eugene, the other waiter here.'

'How long have you worked here?'

She picks at a bit of lettuce which hangs from the side of her baguette and puts it in her mouth, chews a few times. 'A few years, maybe four,' she says, nodding as if agreeing with herself.

'Oh, good. That's good,' I say. I'm not sure what to say next and I think she notices.

'And what have you been doing before this, work-wise?'

'I worked in admin, for a courier company.'

'Bit of a contrast then?'

'Yeah, just a bit.'

She scrunches up her nose, like she's heard some bad news. I must have spoken in a tone I didn't mean to let out.

'Did it all go wrong then?' She doesn't take her eyes off mine.

'Something like that.'

Maybe my expression says more than my words as she makes a face again, this time a look of sympathy, but comically. She's trying to keep the conversation bearable for me.

'Wife and kids somewhere?'

'Just the wife, somewhere.'

'Somewhere,' she repeats with a smile, almost a laugh.

I laugh a little too much. The words, spoken so easily, their meaning so unimaginable, feel almost fictional.

'How about you?' I ask, partly to get the conversation away from me, but also because now she knows something so vital about me, I feel the need to know something about her, too.

'Do I have a wife somewhere?' She raises her eyebrows.

'Well, I meant a husband or boyfriend. But it's a wife, is it?'

I've never met a woman married to a woman before, but I know there are some.

'There's no one, but if there was it would be a boyfriend, maybe a husband, probably not a girlfriend or wife, but who knows?' She puts her baguette down on its plate and picks up her crisps, opens them. 'Don't close doors, that's what I say.'

'Right.'

'But my life's just not that exciting, so the most I'm expecting is a boyfriend. So have you and your wife split up then?'

I look down at the sandwich in my hands, which I've still not had a mouthful of. Ham pokes from its sides. I don't think I can eat now.

'I have no idea.'

She wipes her fingertips on her napkin and then looks at me. 'Want to talk about it?'

I don't. I put my sandwich down. I wish she'd start eating her crisps again; she talks a little less when she's eating.

'No, thank you.'

'OK.' She's not bothered at all.

I feel I've been rude.

'You can help me with one thing though,' I say, remembering what I've been meaning to ask someone for days. 'Do you know where there's a laundrette around here?'

'You don't have a washing machine?'

'No.'

'Well come around to mine and Eugene's and do your washing there.'

'Oh no, thank you though.'

'Yes. Launderettes are expensive. Come round to ours and we'll have some beer, make a night of it.'

'Are you sure?' I ask, grateful for not having to pay for the launderette but even more so for the idea of a night with company.

'Absolutely.'

I feel awkward about accepting, but there's no way I'm not going to.

I walk home in darkness across the heath. The day, and its invite of washing and beer, for which the coming Saturday evening has been decided, has made my mood a little lighter than I've been feeling. The conversation and lunch with Jessica felt like a moment of normality, of relief. I am tired though. I'm pleased for the tiredness, as a full night's sleep would do me more good than beer and washing and company put together.

I lie in bed and think of her. Nothing in the way she asked was flirtatious, and I didn't think for a second that she meant anything other than to help me out with my washing, but an accepted invite from a woman I don't know very well, of any kind, feels strange, even wrong. There's something about the idea of being in her house, in a room alone with her, which makes me feel excitement, but edged with guilt. I want to forget this thought. It's wrong.

I close my eyes and try to disappear into the silence of the house.

FOURTEEN

My friendship with Carl grew as we did. We were getting too old for bike rides and yet were too young to get served in a pub. Instead, we walked the country roads, talking endlessly, and waited outside the shop to ask people to buy beer on our behalf, with varying degrees of success. We still lived next door to each other. His sister Kelly and I had even begun to get along a little. She wrote fiction, and we'd discuss the stuff she was working on as I read more than anyone else she knew. She was working towards completing a novel. She had a boyfriend who Carl and I agreed was far too nice for her. Carl was popular with girls, but he never had a girlfriend, and I never got asked out.

Carl continued to excel at school, while I continued at an average, perhaps a little below average, level. We studied relentlessly for our exams. I struggled with maths more than any other subject, and Carl dedicated hours to helping me. Night after night he'd teach me how to multiply, divide, subtract. Sheets of paper would lie around us, scattered with numbers and scribbles. One night, I finally managed to master long division. He told me to do it again, then again and again. While I worked on one sum, he'd be writing out the next one for me, and each time I did it, I talked him through how I'd done it, as if it was me who was teaching the method to him.

The next day, I couldn't do it, and he began showing me the whole process again.

That summer, we left school and waited for our exam results with great anticipation. When they finally arrived, Carl got nearly straight A's. I got, better than I was expecting, a few C's and a D for maths. 'Only a D?' Dad asked. 'After all that time you put into it? After all that time Carl put into helping you?' He couldn't hide his disappointment, and I don't think he tried to. I wondered then, not for the first time, whether he wished that Carl was his son rather than me. It made me wonder, too, whether my dad who was in heaven would have been pleased with what I'd achieved, but I felt bad for thinking this. Aunt Ruth, however, was full of congratulations for both of us. She bought us four cans of lager to celebrate our success and swore us to secrecy about where they'd come from if we got caught drinking them.

We began Saturday jobs and rode our bikes from Whiteflower to reach them. My job was unloading deliveries for a supermarket. I worked with a team of other guys doing this, with a radio blasting. Carl worked in a shoe shop. We both earned little, but it was our own spending money. Our parents still paid for everything else we needed.

By the time we left school, most people in the village who were around our age had begun to go out more. They'd go to neighbouring villages and towns and try to get served in pubs. They had parties while their parents were on holiday. Carl and I, however, seemed to be turning out a little more quiet than the rest. My passion for reading fiction had grown. I'd read in my bedroom, or in the garden or the woods when the weather was warm. The woods were a wonderful place for reading. There was only the occasional sound of an animal rustling in fallen leaves, birds singing in the bushes and trees or squirrels scrambling over branches. I'd read and doze and then read more when I woke. Time became unimportant. I would just go home when it was too dark to read any longer. It was the only way I could bare to spend time on my own. In those times alone, when I tired of reading, again I thought of my dad in heaven.

Aunt Ruth died very peacefully the day after my sixteenth birthday. From the moment it happened we missed her terribly. She had an illness, so we all knew she would go at some point that year, most likely, but she made her exit before she was too ill, thankfully. I insisted she was buried in her red dress with sequins all over it, which was one of her favourites, rather than the dark blue suit Mum and Dad had picked out, which would have made her look like a businesswoman and she would have hated it. I had to argue with them every day between her death and the funeral but I finally got my way. I thought she would have been proud of me for that. She was buried in a churchyard in Brighton with a crowd of people who loved her surrounding the grave as she was lowered down, gone forever, as gulls circled above and cried as if for her. It all felt so incredibly ceremonious that it distracted me from the enormity of what was actually happening.

I was lost. She was my only relative who felt like a friend. The only person, other than Carl, who I knew I could ask about anything and who I knew could keep a secret. I wish she'd lived longer, so we could have had more time, more laughs, more secret conversations. I cried myself to sleep every night for a week after she passed. My parents tried to console me as best they could, but eventually it was Carl who reassured me that everything was going to be OK.

A strange thing happened, weeks, maybe even a month or two after Aunt Ruth died. I know it was autumn. Dad was out with Carl's dad, buying some new guttering or something. I was lying on my bed, reading a novel about a young man who moved to London in search of fame as a playwright. Mum was in the kitchen cooking dinner. I could hear her banging and tapping and could smell cabbage boiling.

I stopped reading and remembered when Aunt Ruth was dying. The hospital room had been busy with nurses coming in and out, and Mum and Dad were there, but when they turned their backs to talk for a moment, Aunt Ruth said something to me that made no sense, so little sense that I had forgotten about it.

'I can see him,' she'd whispered.

I was about to ask her who she could see, but then a nurse was there again, so I couldn't ask who, and then she died.

FIFTEEN

It's dark.

I have no idea what time it is, but I've woken suddenly. I have no chance of sleep again. I'm awake now, as if I've just jogged or swam, and each time I close my eyes they open again. There's no glow of sunrise and the bird hasn't begun to sing yet. It's outside my bedroom window every morning, in the high branches of the bony tree in the back garden, singing frantically at the first sign that night is ending.

I never sleep for a full night anymore. I sleep for a few hours at the most and then wake up, usually with the dull headache that I feel now. No painkillers seem to touch it. Maybe they don't work with alcohol.

I think of Mia and then try to forget her.

Mia was once my biggest comfort, the source of my contentment. Now, thoughts of her keep me awake and give me nightmares during the shorts spells that I do sleep. I just can't understand how she has left me like this. Though it's me who's not at home, who doesn't return calls, who's in a place unknown, she's left me with no choice, for now at least. I know at some point I'm going to have to make a decision about going there and facing her and Carl, facing all of this. The thought is so awful that I know sleep won't come now. I'm too horribly awake and aware.

I try a new position, turn onto my side and stretch my legs. The new patch of bed feels cold. I must buy a duvet; these blankets are scratchy and thin and smell slightly damp. They might not have been used or washed for years before I arrived here. I will take them to Jessica and Eugene's house when I go there to use their machine.

A door slams. It was out on the landing, either the kitchen, living room, the bathroom or the empty room. I wonder why Mrs Moore would be up in my part of the house again, so deep into the deadest part of night. I lie still, and minutes pass as I listen for the sound of her slow footsteps on the stairs.

Nothing.

Then, a feeling of dread runs through me as to who else it might be. I lean over the side of the bed, pick up my mobile from the floor and hurriedly press random buttons. Its screen illuminates, shows me it's 03:14 and that I have no signal. There's hardly ever a signal in this house. I hold the phone up to the room, which it lightens just a little. I look for any object I might be able to use as a weapon. I still have nearly no possessions except my clothes, which are folded on the floor beside the bed, along with the jumper I found in the loft. The only weapon I have are the fists that I don't know how to use.

I step out of bed and walk across the room with the softness of a bird. I know the door handle will make a noise when I open it. It's old and round and rattly, the same as all the others in the house. I decide I'll make a sudden approach. I'll burst onto the landing and rush into the rooms, switch on the lights, and when I find the burglar I'll kick him in the shins or the balls or the stomach, until he's down enough that I can run from the house. I take a few deep, near-silent breaths.

The lights blind me for brief moments after I switch them on as I run from room to room. All have their doors open and are empty, except for the empty room, where I startle a mouse who startles me and runs into a gap next to the fireplace. The fire there is dying down. I don't remember lighting it tonight. I go back to the landing with my heart in my throat, stand completely still and listen. I hear the clock ticking. The bulb above me buzzes.

I put my trembling hand on the bannister. When I peer down the staircase to where the brightness of the lights diminish into the darkness of the lower floors, I suddenly feel the size of the house and the height that I am within it.

'Who's there?' My throat is dry, my voice frail.

There's no one here.

I walk into the kitchen, pick up the whisky bottle and go to the living room, stand at the window. I look out at the night, but all I see is the solitude of my translucent reflection.

I wake.

It's morning, my headache has worsened and I have the feeling of dread I so often have in the mornings now. I've drunk far too much again and hardly slept. The pain goes across my forehead and spreads back over my scalp. I slowly run my hand through my hair. Every follicle feels sore and I take my hand away. My neck is stiff and I gently try to stretch it. I feel weak and tired all over. The bird sings in the tree outside the window. Its song is piercing. I wish it'd fuck off.

I slowly get out of bed and go to the window, pull the curtain back and the blackbird stops singing. He looks at me sideways, very still, his jet-black eye circled with yellow, like a jewel. His body is stocky and his tail pert. The feathers on one side of his head are ruffled, like he's been wearing a hat. He stares at me and begins his song again, beak open wide, throat throbbing and tail tilting with each note. I tap on the window. His eye widens and he quickly jumps and flies away, leaving a gently bouncing branch behind. The leaves are sparse and beginning to turn brown now.

The dull morning taste of whisky coats my mouth. I go to the bathroom, feeling cool air on my face. This room is always colder than the others. The floorboards have gaps between them and the window frame is rotten. I'll light the fireplace here today. I turn on the tap, cover my toothbrush with paste and look into the mirror above the sink. I notice something on my face and look closer, an inch from the mirror. A dark line runs from one nostril to just above my lip. I wipe my finger across it and some of it flakes away. I never get a nosebleed. I put my finger under the tap and wipe again and again until the darkness has gone away, and I look closely again at my reflection. My cheekbones are protruding. There are slight blue-ish hollows under my eyes and my skin has lost some of its smoothness. People always said I look younger than my age, but I don't think they would now. I look at my green eyes. I've never fully recognised myself when I look into a mirror. I look odd. Even my name doesn't suit me.

I fill my cupped hands with water and splash it over my face, again and again. Streams run down my neck, chest, wrists and arms. I hear them hitting the floorboards but still I wash my stranger's face.

SIXTEEN

We started college together, both choosing Business Studies. Carl thought it would be fun for us to learn about something we knew nothing about, but I was nervous about it at first. We were in some classes together, but for others we were separated again, like in school, by the divide in our intelligence. Starting college, we both felt some independence. We were doing what we wanted. Neither of our parents had convinced us into studying. It was our own free choice, the first major one we had ever made. We were studying for self-improvement and it felt good.

When the bell rang between lessons, the corridors filled with students in seconds. There were five minutes to be made the most of. The flow of bodies rushed in different directions to talk to their friends or queue at the payphone or kiss their lovers. Groups of students would pass a single cigarette and suck and puff as no one could afford sole ownership of a packet. The vending machine would gobble coins, beep and bang out chocolate bars and gently drop bags of crisps as music bellowed from the jukebox in the canteen. A few weeks after we started college, I wandered along the corridor one morning, heading from maths to administration class, when I caught my first glimpse of Mia.

Her head was slightly down, her hair straight, bobbed and pink-ish blonde. She raised her face the moment we passed, looked straight ahead, and I saw her eyes. They were the colour of treacle and glowed like there was a flame behind each of them. I saw the round of the back of her hair, pinker than the front, pink as candyfloss, then felt an anonymous shove on my shoulder. It was only then I realised I'd stopped and turned to watch her, but she was out of sight in seconds and the torrent of people rushing towards their chocolate and friends and kisses and cigarettes were pushing me along the corridor.

After that it seemed she was everywhere I went – at college anyway. I'd see her in the corridors, glimpse her passing by windows and doors, her face there, and then gone, hidden in crowds. I saw her in the canteen getting whistled at, which she pretended not to hear. She parked her bike outside college each morning and chained it to the left gate. Carl and I would arrive at college early and I'd watch her from the canteen window.

Mia was one of the fashion students. You could tell them a mile off, because none of them looked the same. Mia wore skirts, long or short, or trousers or jeans or woolly jumpers baggy enough to hang to just above her knees and seemed to do the job of both top and skirt. Once, I saw her dressed in what looked like a mechanic's overalls, minus the grease. Some days she looked like she was from the 1940s, on other days, the 1970s. She wore a different hairstyle each day, too. Carl said they were wigs, but somehow everything looked natural on her. She always carried books; I'd see their shape in her bag. This made her look more serious than many of the other students. She looked like she was there to learn.

She had a lot of friends, not just the fashion students but from all over the college, mostly girls. Whenever I saw her, I'd always notice the reaction from the male students nearby.

Just by walking to the drinks machine she could silence a crowd of guys. There were other pretty girls at college, lots of them, but none in the same league as Mia. She was a ball of energy. All the girls liked her. Every guy wanted her.

'She must have a boyfriend,' Carl said to me once, as we sat in the canteen.

'Must have,' I said.

I found it difficult to look at her for longer than a moment, in case she caught me looking. I'd hate her to think I was lusting over her, but I also found it impossible not to look. She'd got my attention in a way that no one ever had. It was like she owned me, even though we'd never even spoken to each other. Carl and I would nod whenever we saw her, to check we were aware of her presence.

Carl and I never had any intentions of asking anyone out, going on dates or anything like that, though we were seventeen and most of our classmates were doing so. It was a boundary that neither of us were ready to cross. We'd ended up so alike. Our friendship was as strong as it had ever been. We knew each other so incredibly well, I couldn't imagine having a best friend who wasn't Carl.

SEVENTEEN

I sit in a pub in Blackheath with Eugene.

I was supposed to be with Jessica at their house using the washing machine, but she's now working until closing, and as Eugene had finished his shift at the same time as me, we're having a drink on our way. He sits opposite me with his legs spread wide. He scratches his balls every few minutes. His jeans are fitted and sit scrunched at the bottoms on top of clean white trainers. He smells of a sweet aftershave. He looks like what most people would describe as cool, or trendy or something. He has a small-ish but fit frame. His hair is short, full, dark and gently scruffy. His eyes are dark blue. His movements are springy and his accent is London through and through. He dresses a little younger than his years. His clothes could be worn by an eighteen-year-old hanging out on a street corner, or playing their music loudly on the bus, though he doesn't look silly for it. He looks comfortable. I think me and him are very different.

We finish our pints. He pulls on his jacket and walks ahead of me out of the pub. We walk a few streets on the opposite side of Blackheath to where I now live, down roads of houses, big houses which I imagine families might live in. We stop at a shop and buy cans of beer. It's a nicer neighbourhood than I lived in with Mia. I wish for a moment that we'd lived here together for our marriage.

Jessica and Eugene's house is old, though not as old as mine. It has a homely feel. There are comforts, radiators which Eugene turns on as we go from room to room. Unlike my house, I can tell that people are here, that lives are being lived here.

'Let's get your washing on, mate,' he says, as we stand in the kitchen.

He puts the beers into the fridge, except for two he hands to me and two he takes for himself. We walk up a couple of flights of stairs to where his and Jessica's bedrooms are, opposite each other with a bathroom in the middle. He tells me that others live on the floor below, then shows me his room. It's much tidier than I expected. Organised, spotlessly clean.

Jessica's room is clean but cluttered and smells of vanilla and make-up. There are rugs on the floor, their edges curled. Paintings and drawings of people and views are stuck onto the walls. Eugene jumps onto her bed, lays down and puts his hands behind his head on the pillow.

'Take a seat,' he says, nodding to the armchair in the corner of the room. 'So, are you sleeping with anyone?'

For a moment, I have to think about whether I have heard his question correctly.

He turns to look at me when he notices my delay.

'Not at the moment, no. Are you?' I find myself asking the question even though I have no desire to know the answer.

'Well, there's been a few recently, but no one regular, y'know.'

I decide not to reply at all, in hope of the conversation ending. It works. After a short silence, Eugene pulls out a box from underneath the bed and sorts through the CDs inside it.

'Any preference?'

'Something lively. With the warmth in here I might fall asleep otherwise.'

He doesn't answer and continues to sort through the discs for a while before choosing one and putting it into the player beside the bed.

'This should do you.' He puts on some music that I've never heard before. Thankfully, he doesn't put it on too loud as the music sounds like it belongs in a rave, not that I've ever been to one.

When Jessica calls to say that she'll be leaving work soon, Eugene leaves the room and comes back with a menu, which he studies quite intently.

'We always order from this place. We could just get a pizza each? They're quite big.'

'Sounds great,' I say, despite my loss of appetite.

'Or, we could get a couple of pizzas to share, pasta of some kind, garlic bread and maybe some apple pies?'

'Might be a bit much?'

'Not at all, we'll get through it. Or maybe we should get some salad to go with it? Y'know, like a healthy option.'

'It all sounds lovely.'

'You're not helping, Lewis.'

'Sorry! I'm just happy with whatever, that's all.'

'Oh, and we have to get something without meat for Jess – she's a vegetarian.'

'Really? I didn't know that.'

'It's not normal. Right, I'm phoning. You sure you're happy with anything?'

'Yes, thank you.' I reach into my trouser pocket and take out my wallet, again remembering the photo of me and Mia that's inside, which I still can't look at. It feels like it's following me. 'I'm not using my card at the moment, but if you want to put it on yours I'll give you the cash if that's OK?'

'No,' he holds one hand up in defence and reaches for his mobile with the other.

Jessica arrives just after the pizza delivery, which we've not yet taken out of the bags. Eugene has got several cans of beer from the fridge and puts the pizza beside them.

'I'm home,' she calls up the stairs.

'We're in your room,' Eugene says.

I feel awkward that we've been sitting in here, and I'd not thought how inappropriate it is until now, though Jessica seems unbothered.

She sits on her bed. I'm still in the armchair and Eugene has moved to the floor. We each have a pizza box on our lap. Breaded mushrooms and apple pies lie in open boxes on the floor. Little pots of sauce, the same shade of red as Mia's lipstick, are passed between us and dipped into. I'm eating much more than I expected to.

'Did you get your washing done?'

'Yes, thanks. I have to take it out of the machine yet though.'

'He only had one load,' Eugene says, as though I've fallen short of some high expectation and without looking up from picking crumbs of pizza crust from his T-shirt.

The room is filled with the rustle of bags and boxes and chewing.

'So, how are you finding Blackheath then?' Eugene looks up at me as he speaks now.

'Yeah, it's nice.' I lean down towards the floor and take some garlic bread and he passes the box to meet my hand. I really hope that questions about Mia aren't about to begin. Whereas Jessica asked me if I wanted to talk about it during our conversation in the restaurant, I can't imagine Eugene will have the same diplomacy. 'I need to buy some stuff for the house. The place I'm living in is pretty empty.'

'What kind of stuff?'

'A duvet, towels, cushions, everything really. Except for

the kitchen, as that had everything there when I arrived, though some of it is a bit rusty. The oven's good for a bit of heating though.'

'Is it that cold?'

'Oh yeah. It's got a fireplace in most of the rooms but the one in the living room is boarded up. I need to ask the landlady if I can take the boards off and use it. She's a bit elusive.'

'Ah well, if you need a hand we can come shopping with you. We can go one Sunday when we're all off work,' Jessica says.

Eugene nods in agreement while sucking the tips of his fingers.

All the food has been eaten, and for a moment I think of their generosity. My washing in their machine and the food I've just eaten and not paid for. I feel lucky. I could have been alone tonight in that empty house, just me and the ghosts of Mia and Carl.

With my bag of folded damp washing, I walk towards the village and my headache comes back. I hadn't noticed how it had eased, or maybe Jessica and Eugene had just distracted me from it for a while. Their company reminded me of home. She has some of the caring qualities of Mia. She knows things without them having to be spoken. Eugene also reminds me of Carl at times. I can imagine he'd be a loyal friend, though he hasn't mentioned any friends' names to me other than Jessica. Both of them have opposite sides to Mia and Carl too. Jessica and her confident, single life. Eugene and his promiscuity. He's much more laddish than me and Carl. The kind of guy we'd have nothing in common with.

I'm beginning to shiver. The night is cold. It's quiet too – only the occasional passing car, a couple hand in hand and a fox who walks ahead, stopping to look back at me every few yards. The restaurant is closed, its windows filled with darkness. The pond has sleeping ducks floating on its surface. I like walking at night. I reach my road and pass by the other houses. I stop in front of mine, and gasp.

The house is covered with birds.

They stand on the steps up to the front door and on all the window ledges. A line of them sit wing-to-wing along the gutter; I see their silhouettes against the blueberry sky. Every other house on the road is bare, but number 28 is crowded with crows. I wave my arms and whisper-shout at them, but they just stare, a thousand beady eyes.

I pass slowly up the steps, gently nudging them aside. There's hardly any space for me to walk between their blackness. They jump along just enough for me to place my foot. Some of them look at me with their heads tilted, as if listening, while others stare at the ground, deep in thought. My fists are clenched so tightly that my fingernails dig into my palms.

I shakily get my key in the door and unlock it, slide into the narrow gap and close it quickly behind me. I put the bolt across, locking out the eyes, and begin to walk upstairs with trembling legs.

'Are the birds still here?'

I freeze, and then slowly look over the bannister. Mrs Moore is standing in the hall. She's wearing her usual dark red dress, the yellow glass brooch with the dragonfly set in it and her jet-black hair tied back tight, like every other time I've seen her. Always dressed like she's expecting visitors. Tonight, her eyes are wide and bloodshot and their gaze darts around. She's waiting for me to answer.

'They're all over the house. I've never seen that before. Do you feed them?'

'No.' She pauses, thoughtfully, for a moment. 'I think they're here because of you.'

'Me? Why?'

She reaches up and touches my face. Her fingers feel waxy. 'You look pale again.'

'I've got a bit of a headache, that's all.'

'You had a headache the last time I saw you, and the time before.'

I feel her breath gently puffing on my cheeks. It smells clean, like tea.

'Yes.' I don't want to tell her it's because I'm drinking so much.

'You need to see a doctor. I don't think you're well.'

'I will, thank you.' I continue up the stairs. 'Goodnight.'

'Goodnight, Lewis. Light your fires.'

Upstairs, every room is cold, or maybe I'm just noticing it more after the warmth of the radiators at Jessica and Eugene's.

In the kitchen, I pour a glass of whisky, drink it back in three gulps. I unpack my damp clothes and hang them over the doors, the bannister and over the side of the bath. A scent of summer, though they'll take days to dry in this house. I look towards the window in the living room, but I can't see the birds on the ledge outside. I pull the old wooden frame up on its thinning ropes, lean out and look down to the steps to the front door.

The birds are gone.

I'm relieved to see bare steps. I look up into the darkness of Blackheath. Within the pool of light cast by the streetlamp I see someone sitting on the bench on the other side of the road. I hadn't noticed him on my way in. He's sitting with his back to the houses and the road and is looking out into the blackness, wearing a mac and hat. I wonder why anyone would sit there on such a chilly night. Maybe he's homeless. I feel a little guilty as I close the window, gently so he might not hear.

In the bedroom, I light the fire I made up this morning. I must remember to ask Mrs Moore about giving her money for logs and coal. Stocks of it appear in the shed and I've been taking from it daily. The bedroom is even colder than the rest of the house tonight. On the floor, I see the burgundy jumper I found in the loft and remember the vintage tracksuit I'd found there too. I usually wear it to bed, but it's damp and drying on the living room door. I pick up the jumper, bring it to my face and breathe deeply. It still smells of loft, even though it hasn't been up there for weeks. I hold it up to my chest. It has a low V-neck, could even be a school jumper, but I think it'll fit. I see something written on the label in the collar. I look closely and read the faded letters.

THIS BELONGS TO P.M.

I can't wear today's clothes to bed as I have to wear them to work tomorrow, so I take them off and put the jumper on. It fits. The fire suddenly takes hold, burns furiously like it's been filled with paper. Watching its flames, I feel an overwhelming tiredness and my eyelids become heavy. I go from room to room, switching off the lights and closing the doors, containing the emptiness. Back in the bedroom, I close the door, switch off the light, and in the flashing glow of the fire I get into bed, the tiredness becoming greater every second. The blankets are cold on my legs, but they quickly warm.

I turn onto my side and face the fire. Lying in front of the flames with the blankets wrapped around me reminds me of home in Whiteflower Woods. As I dozed, I'd hear Dad come into my room and throw a log in the fire before he and Mum went to bed. I must call them soon. They'll be worried.

The fire is brilliant. The usually cold room and bed have turned into a place of comfort and warmth tonight. Of home. I relax, knowing for the first time in weeks and weeks that I'm going to sleep well.

My eyes close.

EIGHTEEN

College was the first time in my life I'd experienced change. Though Carl and I were happy in our childhood, now we were in our late-teens we were sometimes finding our home lives boring. We still went for long walks through the woods and fished the lake, though we never caught another golden tench, but we also started to have nights out. We'd go to Brighton some afternoons and not go home until the last train. We couldn't afford to be in pubs for the whole night as we still only had the money from our Saturday jobs, so we'd have a couple of drinks in a couple of pubs and then have a night-time walk along the pebbled beach, with cans of beer swinging from our hands in carrier bags and eating chips from paper soggy with vinegar. Those walks were always my favourite parts of those days.

After we got bored with our trips to Brighton, some Sundays we'd get a train to London. Mum grew up in London and knew it well from her younger years before she and Dad got married and she moved to Sussex, which was where he grew up. She'd recommend places for us to visit. We liked riding on the bus and Tube, but we loved walking more. We got lost all the time. We'd come up with suggestions, seeing St Paul's, going to Camden Market or Covent Garden or walking the streets of Soho. We went into a sex shop for the first time there and had the shock of our lives.

At night, we'd hang around the West End. The atmosphere amazed us. The different types of music coming from different directions. The lights, the shops, the backstreets. We soaked up every bit of it that we could and then usually had to rush for our last train, sometimes sprinting across the concourse of Victoria Station as the guards blew their whistles. There were a few very close calls, though we never actually missed it. It would feel like such a world away, getting home after these times in London, from crowds to space, noise to silence and bright lights to moonlight. When I was back in the quiet of the house in Whiteflower Woods, as I lay in bed alone in the dark and the shadows of the trees danced around the walls, I'd think of Mia.

Our friends at college were talking about moving out of home, whether they were going to go to university and which career paths they might take. Carl and I were still unsure by the time we were halfway through our course. Though he intended to finish it, Carl thought he'd chosen the wrong subject and might go on to study again later. I'd had enough of studying already and knew that once it was all over I would take whatever job came up. Whereas Carl wanted a career, I just wanted a job. It always felt like Carl was the one with a good life ahead of him. My future was a blank page on which nothing significant would ever be written.

We both still got along with our parents well, and though we knew we were living a good life, the idea of our independence was appealing. We talked about where we might move to and thought about the nearest large towns to our village. Then one day Carl suggested London. I think it was as a joke, because we both laughed after he said it, but then we both went a little quiet. A few minutes later we were sorting through the desk in Dad's office, trying to find his diary to look at the Tube map in the back of it, to decide where in London we might look first.

After that, we carried on our college life as normal, though now we had an aim at the end of it. The start of a new life in London. It excited us. We talked about it all the time, and I don't think our parents believed that we'd actually move away from Whiteflower. Mum said that London was the best place for young people to be, but she didn't like the idea of us being so far away. She never really spoke much about her upbringing there.

I was reading a book in the library one day, researching my coursework on how employment laws worked, and I was putting quite a lot of effort into it. As Carl and I were now often in different classes, I no longer had him to show me things all the time, or to lead the way. This brought a change of a kind, because as he was giving me advice from a distance on how I might approach my college work, I found I was beginning to do the same for him. He'd ask for my opinion, or give me an essay he'd written, and I'd give him feedback, and he'd do the same for me. I'd begun to study more on my own, and it was for that reason I was there that day, when Mia walked into the library.

There were a couple of guys at a table close to the door, and as she walked past them and went out of sight down an aisle of books, they nodded to one another and pulled an expression the way Carl and I did when we saw her, though I hoped to God we were more discreet about it.

I went back to looking at my book, though I wasn't reading it anymore. Even being in the same room as her made me lose all hope of concentration. Then I heard her voice, which I'd overheard a few times in the past. Very polite, but direct.

'How are you?'

I looked up to see who she was talking to.

She was looking at me.

'Is there anyone sitting here?' She put her hand on the back of the chair opposite me. Her fingers were long, slim, and her nails were painted purple.

'That's OK,' I said, cringing at the way I hadn't answered her question.

She sat down anyway, gently tucking the chair in a few times beneath her. She smiled at me and I looked back down at my book, which by then might as well have had no words on the pages at all.

'How's your course going?' She put her bag on her lap and began sorting through it.

'Good thanks. And yours?'

'Great, thank you.' She smiled again, then extended her hand. 'My name is Mia.'

Her skin was cool.

'I know. I'm Lewis.'

I realised what I'd said and suddenly blushed so much that I could feel the heat in my cheeks, and when I felt the heat they burned more, until after a few seconds it felt like my face was going to explode.

Mia looked back down into her bag and continued digging through the contents. I watched as her hair, dark brown, straight, shiny and shoulder length that day, fell from behind her ear and fanned over the side of her face.

I clumsily grabbed my books and stood.

Mia looked up.

Unable to bear the exchange any longer, I walked quickly from the library, my legs moving in a peculiar and awkward way that they never had before.

'You *dick*head!' Carl slammed his hands really hard on his temples. He sat on my bedroom floor with an expression of genuine disbelief.

'Well I was put on the spot!'

'Oh my God! That was probably your only chance.'

'I know.'

'And you're absolutely sure it happened the way you told me – that she spoke to you first?'

I had to really try to remember it properly, not because I couldn't, but because it all just seemed so strange, that it felt like it couldn't really have happened.

'Yeah. Yeah, I'm sure.'

Carl looked at the floor. He was considering something. I'd seen this look many times before. He was deciding on whether he should say something or not.

Finally, he spoke.

'You know how she has guys trying to talk to her and stuff? We've seen it a hundred times, right?'

'Yeah.'

'And she has none of it, right?'

'Yeah. What's your point?'

'Well, I've seen her when I've been on my own and she's never spoken to me before. So why?'

'Why what?'

'Why you?'

I had to think for a moment. 'I don't know.'

I really didn't, and again it all made no sense.

Carl stayed until deep into the night. I was so tired that I got under my blankets and laid my head on the pillows as we spoke, and I told him over and over about the library, the purple-painted fingernails, the fan of hair and the coolness of her skin.

NINETEEN

I walk out of Blackheath Village, away from the shops and towards the house I now call home. I think about Jessica and Eugene, about my day at work. I realise there were times when I'd thought about neither Mia nor Carl today. They're with me again now though, like the most persistent ghosts.

I pass the pond, look up and see Parker walking towards me. I feel like I'm beginning to belong here, to be able to bump into someone I know. Though I hardly know him, I'm pleased to see a familiar face. Maybe he has something to ask, or something to tell.

'Hello, mate,' he says.

Stamp recognises me and rushes towards me, jumps up. His little legs only reach my knees and he looks up at me expectantly with his big brown eyes. He's wet from the pond. I reach down and he gratefully tilts his head and pushes it against my hand as I stroke him. His ears are soft, like silk.

'Hi, Parker, how are you?'

'Good thanks. Seems Stamp remembers that favour you did us.'

I'm not sure what Parker means, and for a moment I look at him.

'Our shelter from the storm.'

'Of course, yes. Sorry, I'm not too with it today.'

'One of those days is it?'

'Something like that,' I say.

You have no idea, I think.

An elderly woman is approaching us, with assistance from a younger man. I watch as she comes closer, then I stand to the side of the pavement to make space for them to pass. Parker does the same.

'Oh God,' he says, rolls his eyes and smirks in the way I'd seen him do before, which makes him look mischievous, even though he's not being so.

The woman slowly passes us. Then she stops and turns towards me. She looks at my face closely, the way Mrs Moore does. I take a step back from her.

'It can't be,' she says, moving even closer to me, looking me right in the eyes. She's examining me. Her hand reaches for my face then moves to my hair.

The man looks embarrassed and gently takes her hand off me. I think he must be some kind of carer.

'You've got his face,' she says, quietly. 'Patrick's.'

I look quickly back at her, shudder. I look closely at her now. Her eyes are between blue and grey and their gaze trembles, dances all over my face.

Parker laughs and puts his hand over his mouth.

'My name's Lewis.'

'Sorry,' the man says. He begins to lead her away.

She looks confused, disappointed even, like she's just been told that something wonderful isn't going to happen. I must remind her of someone she's lost. I feel sorry for her.

Stamp begins sniffing around the slow woman's feet. I think for a moment that's he's going to cock his leg up her ankles.

'Stamp!' I call.

The woman turns again, a jolting movement, too sudden for her frail body.

'*What* did you just say?' she asks in a forceful way, like she's about to correct me for swearing.

'I was just calling the little dog away from you.'

She looks down at the ground around her feet, but not at Stamp, who now stands at Parker's side. I think she might be quite blind, and again I feel sorry for her, then she drops. Faints. The young man catches her and gently lowers her towards the ground.

'*Shit*!' Parker says, who's been quiet throughout except for his laugh. 'Let's go.'

'But we can't just leave.'

'There's people here,' he says.

He's right. Passers-by are already gathering around to help. We walk quickly and Stamp trots along ahead of us. I look over my shoulder, but the woman is out of sight amongst all the people.

'She thought I was someone else,' I say.

'Yeah.'

Stamp jumps up the steps to the front door of my house, and then he looks around confused, as if wondering why Parker and I haven't jumped up the steps behind him.

'Oh, Stamp!' Parker says, his voice more despairing than annoyed. I can't imagine he's ever given that dog a telling off.

'Come in for a drink.' The words come out of my mouth before I've even thought about them properly.

I feel stupid now.

'Yeah?'

'If you want to? I need a drink anyway and it's not good to drink on your own – that's what my mum says anyway.'

'Do you always do as your mum tells you?' He smirks again.

I laugh as I realise what I've said, then walk up the steps and open the front door.

Stamp runs ahead of us again, straight up the stairs towards my rooms and waits for us to catch up on each landing. He seems to remember his last visit. He and then Parker go into the living room and I go to the kitchen. I take two bottles of beer from the fridge, go to the living room and see Parker sat on the floor with his legs stretched out wide apart and leaning back on his elbows. He looks quite at home. Stamp does too. He lies on the floor beside Parker, in a sleeping position, and though he opens his eyes and looks up at me as I walk into the room, he doesn't lift his head.

I pass a bottle to Parker.

'Cheers.'

'Cheers.'

We both take a few gulps and then I rest my bottle on the floor beside the sofa.

'I'm sorry it's so cold in here.'

'It's fine,' he says.

But then I realise it's actually not too cold in here this afternoon and maybe even feels a little homely, though I don't know how. It's still bare.

Bottles are emptied and more are taken from the fridge. A crowd of empties sit on the floorboards, one beside me and the sofa and one beside Parker. I've asked him a few times if he wants to sit on the sofa too, but he says he's comfortable where he is on the floor, though he can't be. Stamp is curled up and snoring lightly next to him.

'Why's he called Stamp?' I speak quietly, so I don't wake him with the sound of his name.

'Mum named him. It was something to do with him leaving muddy paw prints all over the house. I don't know how she got Stamp from that, but that's where it came from.'

I wonder about Parker's life, what he does and where he goes when not walking his dog over the heath. Him speaking about his mum makes me think about who he has. There is something in the way he speaks which sounds like his mum is no longer in his life.

'Where do you live?'

'Oh, y'know, here and there. So are you getting used to Blackheath yet? Not your usual grounds, is it?'

He doesn't want to talk about his home life and I don't want to push him to. I do wonder why, though I don't want to talk about mine either, nor the ghosts of Putney.

'Kind of, I think.'

'Are you close to your parents?'

Such a personal question. I don't know where it has come from. I don't like him asking it either, but I feel I want to answer honestly.

'I am, yes. It's my mum and step-dad, though I've been bad at keeping in contact lately.'

'Oh right. You should get in touch with them. Your mum will be worried, I bet. And, if you don't mind me asking, do you think you will get things sorted out with your wife?'

I do mind him asking. I shuffle on the sofa, realise I'm doing so, then stand and walk to the kitchen. I need to compose myself. I get two more beers from the fridge and pretend this is the reason I've left. Parker looks at me doubtfully as I walk back into the living room. Stamp stirs a little, takes a lazy look at me and goes back to his sleeping position.

'Sorry,' Parker says, 'I didn't mean to bring anything up for you. Just thought you might want to talk about it or something.'

I look at him, straight in the eyes, more intently than I have so far, trying to figure him out. A stranger, who must view me as someone quite a lot older than him, who one day sat beside me on the bench next to the pond and asked me for a light and who now sits on my living room floor asking if I want to talk about my problems with him. Part of me wants to know who the hell he thinks he is. Another part wants to say *thank you*.

'Well, I just don't know what to say about it really.' Maybe the beer is starting to have an effect on me. Once I begin talking, the words seem to take less effort than they should to come out. 'I've left her.'

I look at the floorboards.

There is silence. I'm not sure if it lasts for seconds or minutes.

'Why did you leave her?' Parker speaks softly. I notice his change of approach and it makes me want to tell him everything. 'What happened?'

I have to think about if this could really, really have happened, before I can speak. It feels so unreal that I think this must all just be some kind of misunderstanding.

'She was sleeping with my best friend.'

The air goes out of my chest and I can't take a breath. I gasp a little. I'm not breathing. When I snatch a breath it instantly jolts back out and I'm crying. I cover my face to shield it from Parker. I think he sits forward on the floor, as his hand is around the back of my neck and I feel his forearm against my ear. I don't know how long this goes on for, but it feels a long time. I taste tears in my hands.

I'm breathing again, semi-controlled. Parker speaks, but I'm not sure what he's saying. I feel him release his hand from my neck. I have to listen hard, concentrate.

'Just breathe, try to relax. It's OK.'

My hands still cover my face. I don't want him to see it.

'I'm just going to the bathroom. Get us a couple of beers from the fridge will you?' I stand and stumble a little, more from the beer than the upset. We've been drinking for hours and it's night now. The living room light has been switched on though I don't remember either of us doing it. Parker puts his hand on my shoulder for balance as I walk out of the room with my head down.

In the bathroom, I see my reflection in the mirror. I look like I've been beaten up, my eyes are so swollen. My face is red and puffy. I look a mess. How has my life come to this?

I run the cold tap and splash water over my face, but it still burns so I splash more and more until it cools. Then I dry it on the brittle towel which hangs over the door. My skin feels sore and I have to blot it dry rather than rub. In the mirror I still look a mess, but in the calmer light of the living room I hope that Parker won't notice.

Parker is back in his position on the floor, with his legs stretched out and leaning back on his elbows. I lie on the sofa and rest my head on the arm. I'm so pleased he's here. To have company, someone to talk to at night, feels like such a relief.

'You need to look after yourself, Lewis.' He looks at me as if he really means his words, like he's telling more than advising. He talks like an older brother might, but he's years younger than me. I wonder what kind of state I must be in if he's the one who's giving advice to me. It's the wrong way around.

'I need to sleep.' I get up from the sofa. I feel so drunk now. 'Do you have anywhere to stay tonight?'

'Of course I do.'

I don't believe him.

'Well, stay here if you want. You can sleep on the sofa, but I don't have a blanket I'm afraid.'

Parker seems pleased with my offer and is smiling now.

'I don't need a blanket.'

I walk towards the bedroom.

'Goodnight,' Parker calls behind me.

'Night.'

I don't see my bed. I can't even be sure if I walk through the bedroom door.

I open my eyes and the room is dark. I think it's deep in the middle of the night, and though I don't move, I feel even more drunk than when I came to bed. The room is in near blackness, but I can just make out the outline of the bedroom door, slightly open. There's a sound, but I can make no sense of it. I remember Parker is staying and I relax a little, knowing that there is someone else here. I am not alone tonight. I should have told Mrs Moore he was staying. She sometimes still comes up to this part of the house in the night, and when she does I hear her on the landing and stairs, whispering to God.

I lift my head off the pillow, watch the outline of the door and try to concentrate. I think about whether or not I'm asleep, or awake or at some point in-between. Seeing the door and knowing that outside it, a few steps away along the landing into the living room, Parker lies on the sofa, I think I must be awake and that he is awake too. Through the darkness I hear him quietly crying. I wonder why he'd be crying, if he'd told me of anything bad or if anything bad had happened before I came to bed, but my eyes feel heavy and my head drops back onto the pillow.

I wake and sit up startled, like I've just been yelled at. The crazy blackbird is singing outside the window. My head pounds and I lie down again. I'm still not used to hangovers this forceful. I lift my head, slowly this time, and as I look towards the open bedroom door I remember Parker is on the sofa. A feeling of panic invades me and I despair at myself for being so stupid. Letting a stranger stay the night! Panic overcomes my hangover for a moment and I get out of bed quickly. Then I put my hand on my forehead and it hurts at the sudden movement. I remember my wallet, phone, keys, my everything of value and importance. I'd left them out on the worktop in the kitchen, all ready for stealing. I walk out of the bedroom and look through into the living room. Parker isn't on the sofa. I go to the kitchen with my nerves pounding in my chest. Then I see my wallet, phone and keys still sitting on the worktop, along with a ten pound note with change on top of it which I'd taken out of my pockets with them. A little further along the worktop are all of the empty beer bottles from last night, neatly huddled together. Parker must have tidied them from the floor and put them out here, or perhaps I did it myself before I went to bed. I can't completely remember the end of the night.

In the living room, I go to the window. I look out at the cold morning sunlight blasting over the heath and see the back of Parker and Stamp, distantly walking across it.

TWENTY

Mia acknowledged me every time I saw her after meeting her in the library. She'd smile and nod as we passed by each other around college. Sometimes she said hello, or even said my name. I was so happy when she did that. I would have been happy enough that she even knew my name, but to hear her say it! Carl said she was definitely interested in me. I told him that she was just being polite.

Around this time, Carl began to sleep with women. One night at a party, he met a woman who just asked him outright for sex and he did it. We were both eighteen, and sex-wise we were the late starters amongst the people we knew. After his first time, Carl changed a little where women were concerned. Whenever we went on a night out, he'd be hoping to meet someone or get a phone number, and on about half of those nights he got what he wanted. He encouraged me to do the same, but I only had thoughts for one woman. The problem was that pretty much every other guy at college wanted her too, and I knew that I stood no chance at all.

Then one day, in a moment that was just as unexpected

as the first time in the library, Mia approached me again. I was in the canteen, getting a drink out of the vending machine. She asked if she could join me for a coffee. I had to hold the cardboard cup with both hands as we walked over to a table, I was shaking so much, and I knew that once I'd put the cup down on the table I couldn't risk picking it up again as my hands had stopped working properly. In that moment, I actually didn't want to be with her. I wasn't prepared. I needed to ask Carl what I should talk to her about. I looked around the canteen to see if I could see him anywhere, if he could see what was happening, but he wasn't there. Mia sat opposite me, put her bag on her lap and began sorting through the contents of it, just as she had done when we spoke in the library. I watched her, wondering what she was looking for or if she was about to show me something, but then, as I realised what she was doing, I began to relax. She was buying time. She didn't know what to say either and I could see that she was as nervous as I was. Finally, she put her bag down on the floor and looked at me. I knew she wanted to speak, so I didn't say anything. Then, she said the words that changed my life.

'I'd like us to get to know each other.'

It began that easily. Carl told me after that he'd seen it all coming, but it surprised me to the extent that I just went along with it in a state of slight disbelief.

We were just old enough to drink, but instead of pubs our dates were usually walks, films and nights at each other's or mutual friend's houses. There were so many invitations around that time, but most just existed as a crowd of us at someone's house with a few CDs and cans of lager, which would be used as ashtrays when they were empty. Both Mia and I smoked socially back then.

We didn't sleep with each other for a while. I was terrified at the thought, much to Carl's amusement. Mia wasn't suggesting it at first. It wouldn't be her first time, which terrified me even more, as I thought she would have expectations. Carl said it would be an advantage.

People began to know us as a couple. Guys at college would tell me how lucky I was, though one guy started on me once as I walked between classes. He'd wanted to go out with her but she had no interest in him. He was tough and handsome, the kind of guy I, and probably everyone else, had expected Mia to like, but she liked me. She told me so often. We became closer, spent more and more time together. I just tried to enjoy it all as much as I could, as I didn't expect it to last. It felt like we were falling in love with each other, though, when that really did happen later, I realised that we were only just getting to know each other at college. I thought that when she got to know me properly she'd realise there wasn't anything to get to know at all and she'd finish it. I was preparing myself for it, but no such signs came.

As we left college, Carl and I started to look for a flat to rent in London. Mia was going to university there and Carl thought he would have better career opportunities there, or that he might go to university too. I had visions of myself living the life of a Londoner, like I'd been reading in novels for years. After a lifetime in a village, London seemed like the most exciting place in the world. A place where anything could happen.

When we moved, reality sank in. No longer able to go home to my bed in the house in the woods after days out in London, I realised I was part of a machine that never properly switches off. The noise, which is never far away. The crowds. The Tube in rush hour. The being able to do anything or go anywhere at any time of the day or night. Late rides back to the flat on night buses filled with drunk people. I noticed that if I stood in one place for longer than a few minutes, someone would ask me for something, whether it be for spare change, directions or just speaking to me, and I'd not be able to figure out what they were looking for. I learned that when I saw someone unconscious on the street, instead of checking if they were OK, I should just keep on walking.

We lived in a few different parts of London at first. We shared a room in a shared house in Kennington which smelled of damp and, we discovered soon after moving in, had quite a few mice living there too. We were used to mice, having grown up in our houses in the woods, but the ones in London seemed somehow more dirty than those from the woods and we moved out after a few weeks, both feeling quite wimpish. After, we moved to a studio flat in West Ham, which was fine for a couple of months, but when winter began the flat was cold. It warmed just enough to keep the chill away when we had the radiators on but our parents kept warning us how much the bill would be and we got paranoid about not being able to afford it, so we switched the heating on for only two hours at night. We shared a sofa bed there, which seemed OK at first, but we soon got sick of it. As I lay in bed at night in the near dark, I'd look along the cracks that ran across the ceiling, missing the comfort of home and the privacy of my single bed there. Finally, we settled into a two-bedroom flat in Hammersmith once we both had a regular income. It didn't feel like home, but there was nothing to complain about, and after the other places we'd lived in since moving to London, to have nothing to complain about was good enough to keep us happy. Besides, it was only a base for us, a place that stood for our new independence. I got to stay with Mia at her university accommodation sometimes, anyway, and hoped that once she had finished her course we could all live together.

Mia concentrated on her studies, though I still got to see her a lot. She didn't have a job and was living on loans from her parents, so we went to the cinema on cheap nights, had long walks and she came to the flat Carl and I shared. I no longer worried about her leaving me once she'd got to know me. She knew me through and through by then. Those days were easy, filled with fun and passed by so quickly. It was the most optimistic I'd ever felt in my life, those first years in London. I knew good times were happening and that more were coming for me, Mia and Carl.

TWENTY-ONE

I'm in a café in Greenwich with Jessica. It's late afternoon and I've finished my short shift for today. As the restaurant was quiet, Michael told Jessica she could leave too.

I drink tea and she drinks coffee.

I've heard little bits from Eugene and Michael, and sometimes from Jessica herself, that she had quite a full-on career before working at the restaurant. I want to ask her about it. I want to know her more. I don't know if it's a subject she wants to talk about though. Now all general conversation about the weather, the café, the tea and the coffee has passed, I decide I'll ask her. I did, after all, tell her a little about my past, though I didn't tell her what I saw the morning I crashed my car. I think she's guessed some of the stuff I've not told her.

'What kind of work did you do before you started at the restaurant?'

She doesn't hesitate in answering.

'I worked as an accountant, self-employed, for around ten years.'

She really is quite beautiful.

'I worked with my dad first for a couple of years. He had his own small accountancy business. Then I went self-employed. I wanted to study art, but at the time it didn't feel like an option.'

She stops and takes a few sips of her coffee, looks around the café a little. I don't speak as I'm sure there's more of her story.

'So yeah, I worked all hours. Long days, six, often seven days a week. I was earning a lot of money, but I had no time to enjoy it. I bought my own house, just outside of Blackheath, a little two-bedroom place which I was planning on doing up, but I never had time to do that either.'

Again she sips her coffee and again I wait.

'Are you sure you want to hear all this bollocks?'

'Yes. I'm interested.'

'OK. Well, basically, one day I began to close the business down. I recommended other accountants for my customers, sent them to people I knew in the same line of work, and of course to my dad. My parents were horrified when I told them I was chucking it all in because I'd been offered a job as a waitress.'

I laugh and she laughs too, though in a way that suggests she feels that she shouldn't. She covers her mouth.

'I sold my house. I left that whole phase in my life with a bit of money, but more importantly I knew myself a little better. I felt I knew what I wanted to do with my life from then on.'

'So what did you do?'

'Well, I enrolled on an art course. It wasn't that I felt I wanted training, but it helped me network and gave me a bit more confidence in what I was doing. I've sold a few pieces over the past few years, but it's not the money that I'm interested in. I had to learn to live on a budget. I went from having my own place to living in the house with Eugene and the others.'

'Did you and Eugene become friends straight away?'

'I knew him before. He was already working at the restaurant. I'd go in there sometimes and eat on my own and I think he thought I was easy prey. One time I got chatting to him as the restaurant closed and we had a drink together. He asked if he could walk me home, which I thought was very gentlemanly of him. I was impressed. When we got to my house, I wished him goodnight and he said "Can I stay the night?" He asked so politely.'

'And what did you say?'

'No of course! He said he'd never ask again and that I shouldn't be put off coming back to the restaurant because he'd asked. I don't think I said anything at all, but I did fall asleep smiling that night. He has that impression on people, I'm sure you'll have noticed.'

'I can't believe he said that to you. He's got confidence, I'll give him that.'

'He'd ask you if he were drunk enough.'

'What?'

Jessica throws her head back and roars a laugh. Her coffee cup bangs on the table.

We say goodbye at the gates of Greenwich Park and walk the separate pathways across the heath towards our homes. I feel better for having spent time with her, and as I walk I think about how she made me smile and laugh. I'm having good moments again now, though I'm still walking fast so I can get home for a whisky as soon as possible. Sometimes, like now, it's begun to feel like more of a hunger than a thirst.

As I approach the houses on Yarrow Road, I see, for the first time, Mrs Moore outside of the house. She stands at the bottom of the steps with a couple of people who have their backs towards me. A woman and a young man. When I reach them I see that it's the elderly woman who thought she recognised me and called me Patrick and then fainted when Stamp nearly pissed up her ankles.

I nod a hello as I walk past them.

'Hello, Lewis,' Mrs Moore says.

'It *looks* like Patrick,' the woman whispers as I walk up the steps.

I don't look back. I open the front door and go inside, and when I close it behind me I giggle. Mad old cow. I must remember to tell Parker when I see him.

I walk up the stairs, and on the first-floor landing I approach the window and peer out at them. All three of them are looking up at the window. The young man is plain faced, while Mrs Moore has her usual look of worry, but the other woman – she's even older than Mrs Moore, with a wrinkled face and frizzy grey hair – has her hand covering her mouth, as if in shock. She gives me the creeps.

I walk up the other flight of stairs to my rooms, go to the kitchen and take a glass and my near-full bottle of whisky. I sit on the sofa in the empty living room and pour. The edge goes from my hunger and I pour again. I pour and sip and think until the last light of day has gone from the room and the bottle is empty and I realise that I'm sitting in darkness. My head hurts.

Shakily, I stand. The house is silent and then loud with my footsteps on the floorboards as I walk into the bedroom and switch the light on. I'd forgotten I'd made the fireplace this morning. I pick up the box of matches from the mantel and then try to light the fire from the screwed-up newspaper balls, but they burn brightly and then go out and glow orange around their edges. I try again by holding a match against the firelighters. I lose my balance and my hand plunges into the pile of paper and logs and coal. The fire lights. My hand is dirty with coal dust. In the bathroom, I wash my hands with ice-cold water; the hot will take too long to come through.

In the bedroom, the fire has taken hold. The room is filled with the delicate rumble of flames, and for a moment I watch and listen to them.

The smash is enormous.

Glass flies across the room. I turn away and cover my face with my hands. When I take them away, I see shattered glass everywhere, and amongst it on the floor is a bird, lying still.

I kneel beside it. It's a blackbird, the one who sits in the tree outside the window every morning. I recognise it from the scruffy feathers on one side of its head, like it's been wearing a hat.

I pick it up. It's dead. Its chest is warm and its eyes and beak are closed. A wing spreads loose and from it hangs a fan of feathers. I fold it back in place at its side. I'd forgotten the perfect compactness of a bird's wings. It's the first time I've held one since I was very young, and I remember the day Aunt Ruth and I rescued a magpie in the garden from one of her cats. I picked it up and held its bleeding wings by its sides as she scared the cat away. It died despite our efforts and now it rests in the earth in Brighton, like her.

I look at the blackbird's closed eyes. It must have misjudged the tree or got confused with the bedroom light going on maybe, though I've never known that before, not even in Whiteflower Woods, and they were full of birds. The smashed pane in the bottom left square of the window lets in a cold draft.

I lay the bird on the floor. I don't like the idea of it being in the house overnight, and if I leave it outside until tomorrow a fox or a rat might eat it, and I can't allow that. It's the bird who sings loudly outside my bedroom window every morning at the first hope of day, whose voice reminds me that I'm still alive, that I've survived another night. I feel too much respect towards him to let him be eaten from the ground in the loneliness of night.

I walk towards the door, trip and fall heavily onto the floorboards. My hands reach out just in time to save my face. The bird and the smash had sobered me for a while, but now I feel shaky again as I walk slowly up the staircase to the loft, with my hands on the walls for balance. I kneel next to the boxes and sort through the clothes and books. I find a scarf, powder-blue and as soft as hair. I'm sure Mrs Moore won't notice it's gone. The dust is so thick here, she can't have been up here for years.

I wrap the bird in the scarf and carry it to the garden, leaving the back door open to allow a little light. My breath puffs white, but I don't feel the cold. I've seen a spade in the shed where the logs and coal are stored, and I go there and take it, and then begin to dig into the grass. I'll bury him deep so nothing finds his scent and digs him up.

I lay the scarf-wrapped bird in the empty hole. The first spadeful of earth falling onto the scarf makes me shudder, and I quickly throw on another, then another, until the blue is out of sight. I fill the hole and pat gently on the muddy mound to flatten it, put the spade back in the shed and take some logs.

In the bedroom I close the curtains. Then I gather the shards of glass into a pile with my foot. I'll tell Mrs Moore about the window tomorrow. I put the rest of the logs into the fire and change into the tracksuit I found in the loft, which is now fully dry after its washing. The curtains sway slightly in the breeze. I get into bed, pull my hood up for warmth, and as I lay and try to find sleep, I can't stop thinking of the blackbird's closed eyes.

TWENTY-TWO

Carl and I explored our surroundings in London as much as we could. We visited galleries, the theatre and went to the cinema at least once a week. We went on guided history walks and ghost walks, travelled on riverboats and toured historical buildings. We explored, and instead of travelling the long journey home by train to Whiteflower at the end of these days, we'd just get on a bus or Tube back to our place and then drink beer in the evenings. We did go for nights out too and tried out the trendy bars, but we were happier in a traditional pub and found the best ones in the West End, but off the beaten tracks, down the backstreets. They were warm and smelled like The Pheasant in Whiteflower and sold beers on tap that we'd never heard of. We'd try them all, pint after pint, chatting continuously like we had our whole lives and never ran out of things to ask or tell each other. After we'd drank too much, we'd head back to our flat and I'd doze off in bed, with Carl in his room on the other side of the wall, which was the way it had always been really. Here though, instead of hearing the woods outside, birds flapping in the trees or the snap of twigs beneath deer's feet, I'd hear traffic, drunk people yelling at each other and sirens rushing off somewhere.

Mia, in her final year at university, got a part-time job in a florists, which she could fit around her studies. After a few temporary and contract jobs, I'd started in a permanent position in the administration department of a courier company, taking bookings over the phone and assigning a courier to the job. Two years later, I was the department manager, managing a team of three.

I liked the job. It was straightforward, though often very busy. I couldn't have asked for a better team. We did what was required of us and we were mostly left alone in our little office, looking out over the West End, with the radio playing and pizza delivered on a Friday. Work was easy. I felt like I owned something.

Carl worked for a consulting firm in the City. His hard work studying and his skill and enthusiasm for numbers had paid off for him. He liked his job and company and the people he worked with too. After we moved out of the flat in Hammersmith, he moved to Leyton, and though he was renting his flat there, he could have afforded to save a deposit to buy his own. He was earning good money considering his career had only just begun. His flat was nice, had giant candles and vases everywhere and spotlessly clean glass table surfaces. He'd always been a tidy person. Mia and I had been to visit a few times, but he preferred to come to the house I was renting with Mia in Putney as there was more space and we had a garden. He treated it as his second home, which I liked and Mia didn't mind at all. The house felt most alive with all three of us there.

So, early on in his life Carl had achieved a lot and was reaching the goals that he'd set his sights on. He had a few friends, mostly people from work, and he'd go out for drinks with them, but he liked to keep work as work and his private life private.

I said he should meet a woman. Even just dating, he had

such a lovely flat he could take someone home to. He was an eligible man, but something was stopping him. Something was wrong. I thought I knew what it was at first.

TWENTY-THREE

After the quiet of the house, going to work in the restaurant sometimes feels a relief. To come here and see people, hear people, even if it's only taking their lunch orders. I like the walk to work too. Though it only takes five minutes to cross the corner of the heath, I often do a full circuit, from Shooters Hill all along the edge of Greenwich Park to Blackheath Hill, then around to the restaurant. I like to see the football matches and the crows and the joggers of the heath. I like to see its life.

Working at the restaurant has given me an incentive to buy a few items of clothing, because I had none other than those I was wearing when I crashed my car and the tracksuit and jumper I found in the loft. Work gives me a reason to get out of bed each day. I don't think I would do much otherwise, like during my first week or two in the house. When the restaurant is busy, I have no time to think about things at all, and on quieter days, like today, I try to make myself at least look busy. I've wiped down tables that haven't even had diners at them yet. I've watered the plants and taken off their waning leaves and I've dusted all of the spirit bottles behind the bar, twice.

Jessica and Eugene have made a difference to my life too. It feels like they're becoming friends, though I've still not told them properly about Mia and Carl and nothing at all about what I saw them doing together. I think they've figured it out though. It's like they know that something bad has happened but they know it can't be spoken about. They haven't taken any notice of my lack of other friends.

Michael, however, is sometimes difficult to read. When I first met Eugene, he told me Michael was a good guy but a bit of a twat sometimes. Though it's not a description I would give about anyone myself, I've seen what he meant. Michael is sometimes happy or snappy for no apparent reason and his moods can change quickly. I try to avoid him, but in a small restaurant with only two or three staff on at any one time, this is difficult. He looks older when he's in a bad mood, his eyes more deeply set. His voice becomes more forceful and his feet move more quickly, making his entrances into the kitchen or the restaurant loud and unexpected. Today, he's being questioning and a little insensitive. I think it might be because there were only five customers in over lunch and we've taken less than forty quid from them. He's been threatening lately to send us out into Blackheath Village with leaflets telling about our lunch deals.

'So, why *are* you here in Blackheath then, Lewis? We were wondering this the other day.'

It annoys me that he's said *we*. He can only be referring to Jessica and Eugene, though I'm sure it's Michael himself who was wondering and no one else. I'm not sure if he's said it deliberately to make me feel like they are talking about me.

'I've had a few problems at home and am now having a bit of a trial time away.'

'A trial.'

'Yes.'

He looks at me. I try to show that I'm confused as to why he might be asking, but I'm no good at pretending anything and I feel myself blush. He keeps looking at me, so I busy myself wiping a cloth over the table next to us, even though I wiped it just now and its surface is still smeary wet.

'I always find the word trial such an interesting word, in these circumstances.'

I say nothing.

'You said you were local when you first came for the job. Where are you living?'

Now I know he hasn't been discussing it with Jessica and Eugene, because they know where I live.

'Just over there' – I point towards the window – 'Yarrow Road.'

His face softens a little. 'Nice location.'

'Yes, and I have nearly the whole house to myself too. The landlady, Mrs Moore, only lives in the lower ground floor and it's a big house.'

He laughs and then takes my elbow and leads me out of the door. It makes my heart race as I don't know what's going on. He looks across the heath and points to Yarrow Road, towards the house where I live.

'You live there, in number 28?'

'Yes. Why?'

'I know her. She's crazy.'

'Maybe a little.' I feel bad for saying something negative about Mrs Moore.

'She's well known around here. Ask anyone who's lived here a few years. She's made quite a mark here in her life.'

'You've got the wrong person.'

'No. Mrs Moore, number 28. It used to be the most notorious house on Blackheath, I'm telling you. All the stuff that used to go on there and some of the characters that used to rent those rooms, unbelievable. Until the accident. Then hardly anyone saw her after that, poor cow.'

'What accident?'

'It's strange. I'd not seen her around or even heard her name for so long. I thought she'd died or something.'

We look across the heath to the house. Someone is sitting on the bench on the edge of the grass opposite it. I'm sure I've seen them sitting there before. The sun has been hidden behind an almost complete covering of rough, light grey clouds and the tree-ish thing which grows from the gutter is swaying in a new breeze.

'No, she's still there.'

For a quiet moment we just look at the house, then Eugene appears running across the heath towards us. I'd noticed he was late for his shift, but I didn't think Michael had, though now he looks at his watch.

'Oh, that fucking boy,' he says, turning and walking back into the restaurant.

I smile, and when Eugene sees, he laughs, slows his run to a walk and sticks his fingers up at Michael's back.

TWENTY-FOUR

Sometimes, when I looked at Carl, I'd see in his expression, or maybe in his eyes, that his mind was somewhere else. He'd have a concentrated expression, like he was studying numbers or words on a page, but instead of a page he was staring into space, at the floor or at some part of his body. When I'd say his name, or if he realised I was looking at him, he'd snap out of it and instantly be back in the room. I mentioned it to him, but he'd just say he was daydreaming and never reveal any more than that. He never used to do this when we were kids or teenagers. It started later on, though I don't remember any specific time that I first noticed it. I thought that, as we had been close for all of our lives, maybe he felt a bit lonely now that I lived with Mia and had told him I wanted to marry her.

We'd joke about how we were getting older, even though we were only in our twenties. It did feel like we were older though. Things had changed. Carl worked longer hours than me and his job was more stressful, but he seemed not to be worried about that. After I had finished work for the day I would go home to Mia and I noticed on the evenings when we didn't see Carl that he was going home alone most of the time. I would text or call for a chat with him, as I never felt comfortable with the thought of him having to be alone. It felt odd. Other than the times when I saw him daydreaming, Carl was always happy. He was the endlessly positive one out of the two of us. He began going to the gym and eating more healthily. It only took a few months before a difference began to show. His arms and shoulders became more bulky and his chest more round. He'd run in the park in the mornings before he got ready for work. When he stayed at our house, I'd see him come back after these runs, his T-shirt drenched in sweat and telling me he felt great and that I needed to start joining him. I liked the thought of it, but I never had the energy or enthusiasm for things like Carl did. Once he sets his mind on something, he does it. I always said I would run with him, that I would start the next day, though it never happened. To anyone who didn't know him like I did, he'd just seem a nice guy with a good job and a decent flat, with everything going well in his life and with no reason at all to be anything other than the happy person he appeared to be.

As time passed, I began to realise that something was definitely wrong. I told him about this and he told me not to be so silly, that nothing was wrong, and that if there was, what reason would he have not to say so? For the first time in our lifelong friendship, this caused a little divide between us, because I knew that what Carl was telling me wasn't true. It was such an alien thing that it stood out, instantly, and I looked at him very closely. He knew that I knew he hadn't told the truth and there was something deep going on behind his eyes in that moment. He looked as though he was about to fall apart on the outside and like he already had on the inside.

I spoke to Mia about it, who said that Carl was a grown man and didn't have to tell me everything, that maybe it was something personal. This surprised me, as she knew the friendship that Carl and I shared. It made me feel that she just didn't get it. I couldn't understand how she couldn't see a change in him; she had known him for years and the three of us had spent so much time together. She said that he did daydream, but that everyone does. I knew she was wrong about him, but I had to leave it. I thought maybe she was right, maybe it was something personal, though I couldn't imagine for the life of me what it could be. I couldn't think of anything that could be affecting him so deeply but that he couldn't tell me. Nothing about him would have shocked me.

Life continued. Long, fun days out, nights at home or drinking in pubs, birthdays, anniversaries. The three of us learning to drive and Mia and I buying our first car. Weeks at work and counting down the days to holidays. Our lives continued to roll onwards and they were happy for us – three young people living in London. But every now and then I'd see it, sometimes feel it. I'd see words behind his eyes that he wanted to say, but couldn't.

Carl had become a man with something on his mind.

TWENTY-FIVE

Michael had been in a tricky mood all day yesterday. I avoided him, whereas Eugene was trying to wind him up: he dropped things when he never normally does and asked constant, unnecessary questions. I tried to stay out of both their paths in the end, as Michael was making me nervous and Eugene making me laugh when I shouldn't have been doing so. I smile as I think about it now, as I sit on the steps outside number 28, waiting for Jessica and Eugene to pick me up in a car they've borrowed from a friend. It's Sunday, so we all have the day off work as the restaurant is closed and we're going shopping for things to make my new home look like someone lives here. I don't have much enthusiasm for it, but the rooms are so bare and I want them looking better so I can invite the two of them around sometime. It would feel like such an achievement, being settled and being able to invite them around for dinner.

It was Jessica who suggested our shopping trip again. I hope she hasn't done so because she feels sorry for me. The thought makes my smile fade. I know Eugene isn't coming because he feels sorry for me. It's because he's excited about driving a car, which he told me yesterday he hardly ever does as he can't afford to buy and maintain one.

I have two hundred pounds in my wallet, and I travelled into the West End last night to take it out of a cash machine so that Mia can't see I'm living in Blackheath when my statement comes through at the end of the month. I really need to sort out a new bank account which she won't know about. Michael has agreed to pay me in cash until then.

I hear the roar of an engine and then a screech of tyres as an eighties-looking, dirty dark blue car skids to a standstill in front of me. Jessica waves from the passenger seat, smiling broadly, then gets out.

'Hi, Lewis.'

'Hello.'

'Jump in,' she says, pulling the seat back to let me in.

I hesitate, realising it's the first time I've been in a car since I crashed mine. I'd not even thought about being a driver or even just a passenger in a car again, until now.

'What's the matter?'

'Oh, nothing, nothing at all.'

Eugene looks at me quite seriously as I crouch down in the back seat, holding both his hands on the steering wheel. He's wearing sunglasses, even though it's been cloudy all morning and is forecast to be like that all day.

'Hello, gorgeous boy,' he says.

'Hi.'

'Take no notice of him,' Jessica says. 'He's been acting like a dick since we picked up the car.'

'Nothing new there then.'

Eugene looks at me with a mock-shocked expression, leaning his head down to look over his shades, then puts his foot down and turns to face forward a few seconds after we've shot off at speed. My hand scrambles over my shoulder for a seatbelt.

We drive to Croydon, at Eugene's suggestion, and walk around a home store with a basket each. They put things in their baskets and ask me after if I like them, as if the things are for their own place. Jessica has chosen a light green throw for the sofa and has now picked up a chunky white candle. She holds it near her face and breathes deeply.

'We should get a couple,' she says. 'They're vanilla. They'll help get rid of any damp smells.'

I haven't even noticed a damp smell, but I suddenly think that maybe my clothes smell of it. I grab the shoulder of my tracksuit top and sniff it when neither of them are looking. I think it's OK. I can just smell the scent of flowers that is always in the living room.

Eugene is being much more practical than I expected. In his basket there is a small cutlery set, duvet and pillowcase covers and a bath towel.

'You need all this shit, right?' he says, holding the basket up towards me.

'Yes, I do, all of it. Except the cutlery.'

'Oh, right.' He takes the box of cutlery out of the basket and puts it on the shelves full of towels.

I don't pick anything out as I follow them around. They feel parental today, choosing things for me and driving with me in the back seat of the car, and I feel some relief at this, at being led. My legs are aching and I'm hoping we can go soon, but they continue at a slow pace, picking things up, holding, touching, sniffing, asking me what I think of things until every part of the shop has been covered and I'm exhausted.

At the checkout, the items come to £120.

'You didn't get much really.' Eugene is packing things into carrier bags with Jessica while I pay.

'I guess it's a start.' I feel disheartened at hearing myself say the word *start*. It feels like such an awful place to be. I don't want to start again.

The shopping bags sit beside me on the back seat as we drive to Blackheath. Eugene's driving has improved since earlier. Maybe his excitement has worn off a little. He drives more carefully now, with just an occasional, sudden burst of speed to make a traffic light or to stop people cutting in.

'Have you told Lewis about his surprise laptop?' He doesn't look at Jessica as he speaks and his eyes stay on the road through his sunglasses.

The sun still hasn't come out.

'Well it's not much of a surprise now, is it?' She slaps him on the leg, but it causes no reaction. She turns to look at me.

I feel embarrassed.

'My parents got me a new laptop for my birthday this year and I'd not long bought a new one for myself, so I was going to give you that one.'

'Oh, thanks, but you can't give me a laptop, they cost a lot of money.'

'But I haven't paid for one of them, have I.'

'Yes, but still, I'd have to pay you for it.'

'I told you we'd have this shit.'

'Shut up, Eugene.' She turns back to me. 'Well, you're not paying me for it, and it's in the boot for you so when we drop you off with your shopping I'll give it to you then. It'll keep you occupied until you get a TV sorted. You can listen to CDs on it too.'

'I don't know what to say.'

I really don't either, and as she's finished what she has to say and Eugene is lost in driving, we sit mostly in silence for the rest of the journey back to Blackheath.

I put the shopping bags on the kitchen table and go to the cupboard for a glass and bottle. I've been OK without a drink today but it's been on my mind and I've been looking forward to getting home to have it, like I used to look forward to dinner. I don't think I'll have any food tonight. I'm not hungry at all.

I take the blue towel from the bag and bring it to the bathroom, shake it so it's folded in two, then hang it over the side of the bath. It'll be much nicer to use than the scratchy towel I found in the loft. I put the chunky candles on top of the mantel in the living room, as it's the only place to put anything in here other than the floor. I hadn't thought today about buying anything like a table, and Jessica and Eugene probably don't realise I have hardly any furniture. I put the plant that Jessica chose in the bathroom. I think it'll do well in here, as the room is so bright. Hopefully the cold won't kill it. The house is bound to get even colder as winter creeps on.

I leave the rest of the shopping in the kitchen and take the laptop into the living room. It is a little bigger than the one we have at home and it feels awkward and heavy. I press the power button and a gentle roar of tiny fans inside it fills the otherwise silent room. It's dark outside now. I'm sure the silence of this house gets deeper as the light goes from it.

I click onto the internet and the page immediately reminds me that I have no internet connection. I hadn't even thought of that, and I doubt Jessica had either. I look to see what Wi-Fi connections are available. There's one, which shows me the connection is unlocked and that there is one, then two bars of signal, which is one more than I get on my mobile in this house. I connect to it, then Jessica's homepage appears on the screen, a shopping website showing a delighted-looking woman wrapping a coat lovingly around herself with £29.99 half stamped over her, and I feel relieved, so very relieved, at this connection from the house to the world outside, a window to life sitting on my lap. I drink as I browse into the darkest part of night.

TWENTY-SIX

Being in love with Mia changed me.

We'd look each other right in the eyes for a few seconds at unexpected moments and see a look of recognition. Those seconds would last in my mind. It was a new sense, like touch or sight. I felt an awareness that I'd never felt before. Maybe it was something that was lying dormant within me, within everyone, but a few seconds in her eyes and it came to life. It woke.

It made me more aware of life and, in turn, death. One day this feeling wouldn't exist anymore, and knowing that made me feel a sense of gratitude I'd never known before too. I was thankful I'd got to experience it, for knowing about love. I'd always thought of love as a light-hearted thing, something said as a kind of comfort or scribbled quickly into a birthday card, but her recognition made me realise its truth. It existed, and one day death would come, the only thing that could ever take it away. Our bones would lay separated and alone without knowing anything about love. Loving her made me appreciate life. On my mind day and night was if or when I should ask her to marry me. If she said *no* then everything would be ruined. Thinking about it stopped me from sleeping and from concentrating properly at work.

One morning we were in the garden. Mia was showing me a nest that the thrushes had started building in the oak tree. She was wearing a pair of my shorts and a T-shirt, which she always wore as we ate breakfast. She took me by the hand and led me across the lawn in her bare feet, and as she stood under the tree and pointed up, the question came out. She asked me. Her words were confused and mixed up, like she couldn't speak English very well. I said *yes* and she burst out laughing and jumped on me and we fell to the ground.

The following year, we married on an April day so comfortably cool and brightly sunny that it seemed God was everywhere we looked. That's what Mum said anyway.

An hour or so before the ceremony, Carl and I arrived at the church, and as I stepped out of the car onto the pavement I was so nervous that I felt sick. Having had hardly any sleep hadn't helped. I'd spent the night at Carl's flat. We'd stayed up much later than planned and talked for hours and hours, drinking shandy so as to avoid hangovers. I was nervous even then, not of getting married but of the day itself, of being half the centre of attention. Carl was trying to put my mind at rest. We went through everything that was going to happen, over and over again. He's always had a way of putting things, of making things sound better or easier. He's such an incredibly optimistic person. I'm sure that even on his deathbed he'll find something positive to say about the situation.

Carl insisted on me sleeping in his bed on my own and him sleeping on the sofa, but after a short doze, maybe an hour or less, I was awake again in the depths of the night. I could hear the gentle ticking of the alarm clock beside his bed and the occasional footsteps of people outside. Lying in Carl's bed made me think about him, the life he lived and the bed he slept in alone. I wondered what he thought about when he lay there in the middle of the night when he couldn't sleep. The following day, when I married, the times in life that we had shared would take a small step of separation. I'd always thought that a friendship could be as strong as a relationship, but loving Mia made me realise that love wins. I'd marry Mia and the paths which Carl and I were taking would change. I wished that he would meet someone and fall in love. I wanted it to wake in him, too. I lay in the darkness until the first blue-ish signs of day filled the room.

Knowing that sleep was nowhere near, I got out of bed and walked through the living room, quietly so I didn't wake him, and went to the kitchen. I switched the kettle on, turned and jumped with shock as Carl walked through the door in the near darkness, asking if I was making him one too.

We sipped our teas and watched from his balcony as that day's spectacular sun emerged over the rooftops of London.

TWENTY-SEVEN

I wake aching for Mia. It's cold and I'm curled like a ball, wrapped in the blanket, and my head hurts. I see the first signs of day through a gap in the curtains. The blackbird is singing outside my window.

I rub my eyes, confused. I remember the dream about him smashing through the window. I try to remember when the dream was. A few days ago. A week, maybe. I think of the flawless detail of his feathers as I picked him up and his wing fanned at his side. The warmth of his chest. I think of how many times I've heard him singing outside the window since. This might be the first morning, or it could have been every morning. His singing has become such a part of my daily wake-up that it's difficult to think of when exactly I last heard him. He's always there.

I hold my hand to my head. Then I see the little pile of broken glass on the floorboards that I still haven't got around to clearing up. I get out of bed, walk slowly to the window and gently lift the curtain. The bottom left pane is missing. Only jagged edges around its frame remain. I lift the curtain fully and the singing stops. The blackbird with the scruffy head is on his usual branch. He looks at me wide-eyed before flying away. I pull the window up and a few of the jagged edges land tinkling onto the back-garden path. I peer out, look down to where I buried the blackbird and see a small patch of freshly turned earth on the grass. It hasn't been dug up, but it makes me feel uneasy and I close the window.

I put the kettle on, and while it boils I look out over the heath. Looking from the front of the house rather than the back makes the uneasiness go a little, but I still think of the bird. The softness of his feathers. The perfect compactness of his wings. His dead, closed eyes.

The kettle clicks off and I make myself two cups. I feel so dehydrated after last night's whisky. My head is throbbing, badly, like most mornings now. I take one of the cups into the living room and look out over the heath again. Daylight is fully here now, the sky completely covered with dull white clouds.

I finish the first cup, put it in the sink, take the second and go to the bedroom. I'm lucky that it's not been freezing with that hole in the window. It's November, but the last few nights have been mild. Frosts will be coming soon.

It must have been flying fast to hit the glass hard enough for a bird of that size to smash through. It's so strange that any bird would have been flying in the dark of night. They just don't do that. I feel uneasy again as I look out into the garden. A little sick even. Last night's whisky and this morning's tea feel like they're mixing together.

I go to the bathroom, the room that always feels the most bare. It's this room, more than any other, which reminds me that I live here alone. I lit the fire one night before I got into the bath and never cleaned it out again after. A pile of black and grey ashes remain in the shape of small, overlapping logs.

I turn on the taps of the bath, the hot on full and the cold on halfway, and put the plug in. I pour my tea down the sink, unable to stomach anymore. I watch the rising line of water in the bath, rising, rising, until I hear it begin to pour through the overflow. I turn off the taps and run down the stairs, jumping two and three at a time. I'm so sure it was the blackbird with the scruffy head that I buried. I remember the fluffy feathers sticking up on his head as I held him.

I open the back door, step out into the garden and feel an overwhelming sense of grief, such an immense feeling of loss, that there's an instant lump in my throat and I find it difficult to see. It's dizzying, a horrible drunkenness, as if the ground, maybe even the sky, moves. I cover my face with my hands until it stops. When the world stops again, I find my way to the shed and take the spade.

I dig, feeling the sharpness of the spade through my socks. I dig the earth fast and hard, then more softly as I think I get deep enough. I dig further, deeper, much deeper than I remember. Then I see the blue scarf. It's dull and damp with mud now. I squat beside the hole, gently take the scarf out and rest it on the grass. A few slow breaths and I begin to unwrap it.

My muddied hands reach over my mouth as the lump in my throat melts into tears that begin to flow uncontrollably down my cheeks. I feel the dew of the grass soak through to my knees, look down at the dirty scarf and the muddy photo, the photo of me and Mia that has always been in my wallet.

'What have I done?'

I cry gut-wrenching sobs as the first sun of the day shines down on me through a new gap in the clouds.

TWENTY-EIGHT

On the morning of my wedding, Carl and I ate a fried breakfast at a café, then went back to Carl's flat to shower and dress. We sprayed and scrubbed and moisturised like never before, laughed at how we were doing so. Carl spent a long time styling my hair. I preferred to have a short cut and then let it do its own thing. It never sticks up or looks messy. Carl always gels and spikes his hair and said that morning that I should do the same. He said that as best man it was his responsibility to make sure I looked good, that it was important that everything was perfect. We both wore dark blue suits, mine with a pale blue shirt and his with mauve. He brushed our suits again and again, even though I could see no dust on them.

Later, with my hair wet-looking and vertical and very slightly leaning to one side as if someone had blown the spikes down with a big puff of air, which he had, we walked amongst the graves of the churchyard. We stopped at some and read their inscriptions. Names, dates, relationships, lives, but the letters were fading and the facts eroding, becoming covered with ivy and moss.

Carl was a little quiet. As we'd got ready, he'd been excited about the day ahead and was teasing me about the married life I had to come, but then, after the car had arrived to pick us up, during the journey he calmed, became contemplative. My nerves had returned, good nerves now, excited nerves. As the guests began to arrive, Carl became lively again, as if remembering his role, but his words, even his movements, were sluggish.

After all the planning, I was relieved to see everything falling into place. People arrived in good time, all dressed up and smiling, everyone smiling. Relatives and friends who had not seen each other for years exchanged hugs and kisses. People who had never met shook hands and introduced themselves to each other. Church bells were ringing. There was a feeling that what was about to happen was enormous. It meant a great deal to me that everyone was there to watch Mia and I get married. The day was becoming all I'd ever hoped it would be. I was so happy, and I really, really had to remind myself that it was all actually happening. All I could think of was how I had been so very fortunate.

Carl and I were near the altar. We had been told that Mia was outside the church and that the ceremony was imminent. The enormity of it all flooded my mind in those few minutes I was waiting. I was twenty-four, the same age as Mia. Carl was just about to turn twenty-four. I was overwhelmed with everything that had brought me to this proud point in my life, all the memories and people, so many of whom were there in the church. I imagined Aunt Ruth sitting in the front pew. I could feel her love. I thought about my dad. The one in heaven. I felt his presence too, and again I had an immense feeling of appreciation.

A sudden silence fell, followed by a coughing and clearing of throats as if many of the guests were about to make a speech. As the organist began to play, my legs began to tremble and I felt an enormous pressure of eyes focussed on the back of my head, though everyone was probably looking at Mia. I turned to Carl. I needed a look or word of reassurance, but he looked at me confusedly and he'd gone pale, his skin the white of death, making his blue eyes as bright as a blackbird's egg. He looked as though he'd seen a ghost, not me, standing beside him.

'Are you OK?' I whispered.

For a moment, he just stared at me.

'I think it's supposed to be me looking after you today, Lewis.'

His smile wasn't real. Then he looked to my side and I turned and Mia was standing there. I lifted her veil, cobweb-fragile, and she was beaming beneath it. We exchanged our vows of lifelong companionship and protection and love, both of us nervously stumbling over our words. Then Carl passed me the ring to put on her finger.

TWENTY-NINE

Eugene and I have a pint each on the table in front of us. Tonight, the pub, and Blackheath in general, is quiet. I've felt ill for days and have just about managed to get through work. All I wanted to do after was go home, but tonight he's insisted on a drink. I'm relieved that he does most of the talking.

Eugene has sex all the time. His life is a random mix of experiences, most of them pleasurable by the sound of it. He doesn't take anything in life seriously. I find myself wanting to gently shake my head at him.

'I'm a free man, and London is a wonderful place to be a free man,' he says.

Just for a little while, I'd love to see life through Eugene's eyes. Mia is the only woman I've ever slept with. She's the only woman I ever wanted to sleep with in my entire lifetime. I've wanted other women, but I've always known the difference between fantasy and reality, and that's where Eugene and I are so different. He has chosen the life of fantasy.

When Mia and I were twenty, we were going to the

theatre and having nice meals for nights out. I'd see other people our age, dressed more fashionably, with lovers hanging off their arms. They threw up in gutters and drank beer from cans at bus stops, wearing no jackets on the coolest of winter nights, their breath white and puffy in the air as they laughed. I'd see their happiness and abandon as we walked past them like a middle-aged couple. I saw that there was another life going on, but I had my own.

Eugene leans back in his chair, stretches his legs wide apart. His T-shirt is well fitted around his chest and arms. He's in good shape. I can see why woman are attracted to him.

'Do you go out much, Lewis?'

'Not really, no. Sometimes I walk to Greenwich and sit in a café or a pub there and read the paper, but no, I don't really go on nights out much.'

'How come?'

I feel stupid for saying *Because I don't want to*, which is the first thing that comes into my mind. I'm not sure it's the truth anyway. It's because I don't have anyone to go with now, more than anything.

'Ah well,' I say.

Eugene looks at me confused, still waiting for an answer.

'I just don't seem to get around to it. And I've just separated from my wife. Bit of a funny time at the moment.'

'Even more reason to get yourself out there. How long has it been since you slept with another woman?'

I think carefully about my answer.

'A very long time,' I lie.

'There you go then. Next time you're at a loose end, let me know, we'll hit the West End.'

I'm always at a loose end. My whole life is a loose end now. The thought of being on a night out with someone as manic as Eugene just makes me want to sigh, but somehow, something is pushing me.

'OK. OK, thanks, I will.'

I lie on the sofa, feeling more alone than ever.

Maybe it was hearing of the excitement of Eugene's life, or maybe as time goes on I'm just becoming lonelier. My body feels odd tonight, too. I have a slightly numb feeling in my legs and, strangely, my wrists and hands. This feeling has been coming and going lately, but tonight it's lasted for hours. A feeling of persistent weakness, like I'm ill.

I have another feeling I've not had before. I want to see Parker. A guy at least ten years younger than me, likely still a teenager, who I barely know and who may not think anything of me at all due to us hardly knowing each other. Lately though, the smallest connections with people seem to mean a lot. I feel silly for it.

I go to the kitchen, take a bottle of whisky from the cupboard and pour a full glass. I'll text Jessica to ask if she's up for a chat on the laptop. I know she'll be home from work by now. She's set me up on some video-chat thing. Speaking to her might make the night go more smoothly, might make me feel better. I feel uneasy tonight. I'm still uncomfortable about the photo I dug up in the garden and how all that happened. There is a pile of broken glass on the bedroom floor, but the blackbird is still alive. I decided that morning that I was going to stop drinking, but I only lasted until that evening.

I have one little bar of signal on my mobile. It's always the same in this house. Sometimes even the one little bar isn't there and takes hours to return. I hold the phone up towards the ceiling and, after a few attempts, though the bar disappears, the message sends.

I lie on the sofa again, put my glass on the floor beside it and switch the laptop on. While it starts up, I go and get the bottle from the kitchen. It'll save me having to go back out for it while I'm chatting to her. The house is so silent tonight. I can even hear the little fans in the laptop as I walk back across the landing, like the sound of vacuum cleaners working in another house.

A static, blurry image of Jessica appears on the screen. As she becomes clearer, I see the jumping of her hand as she waves, as if her hand disappears then reappears in a different place.

I wave back.

'Can you see me?' she asks, her words piercing through the quiet room, lips slightly out of sync with her voice, but then it all catches up and Jessica is looking very expectantly from my screen, which makes me laugh a little. She looks relaxed, wearing a hoody, which I think she might have had the hood pulled up on before as her hair is messy.

'Yeah. You see me?'

'Yep!'

'Success.' I lie full length on the sofa and position the laptop on my legs. I can see her bedroom behind her and recognise her paintings on the walls from when I visited there with my washing. I hadn't known then that she had painted them herself. I'll look more closely next time I'm there. It felt so much like a home, their place. 'Have you got anything to say then?'

'No,' she says, laughing. 'You got anything to tell me?'

'I got some food shopping earlier. Oh, and I had a pint with Eugene.'

'He's already told me that. Is that it? Blimey, I'm gonna have to switch the telly back on in a minute!'

I laugh. I'm so pleased I asked her for a chat.

'He got a last-minute date and he's just gone out.' She rolls her eyes.

'Oh, really? Who is it now?'

'Not sure. She came to pick him up. I looked out the window but couldn't really see into the car. He was texting her for a while tonight, and when I asked him about her, he was a bit elusive. He's got something to hide.'

'Got a lot to hide I should imagine.'

'He went out just now wearing so much aftershave that,

well, if I was to have lit a match in front of him, he'd have gone up.'

I laugh. 'He must be trying to make an effort for whoever she is then.'

'I know. What a dick!' She laughs, then leans a little closer to her screen, her eyes squinting. 'Oh, have you got someone there?'

'No, just me here, and Mrs Moore downstairs, I expect. I hardly hear her, to be honest.'

'Well who's that man standing in the doorway then?'

I leap off the sofa. The laptop bangs onto the floor and whisky spills and I look behind me. There's no one there. Somehow, the doorway looks even emptier than it should. My heart is pounding so hard that I'm struggling to breathe.

I don't take my eyes from the doorway, lean down to pick up the laptop and glance at it, expecting the screen to be cracked. It's not, but it's black. I press the power button. It begins to start-up again and I leave it on the sofa, barely taking my eyes from the door, and take my mobile from my pocket. No signal. I had the one bar in the kitchen when I texted Jessica. I try to calm myself, and then I walk to the door.

I look up and down the landing as if waiting to cross a road. It's empty. If anyone was here I would have heard them. The floorboards creak everywhere, as they do under my feet now. The bedroom, bathroom and kitchen are all empty. The mouse who lives in the empty room isn't even at home. My heart is beginning to slow now, though I still breathe like I've been running.

I fill my glass again, pick up the laptop and sit on the end of the sofa, positioning myself so my back is to the window and I'm facing the door. I'm too nervous to take my eyes from it for longer than a few seconds. I connect to the internet and soon Jessica is back on the screen. She looks panicked.

'What the hell just happened, Lewis?'

'You made me jump and I dropped the laptop!'

'Who have you got around there then?'

'No one, it's just me.'

'What?'

'Seriously. There's only me here.'

'But I saw him. I hadn't noticed him at first, but he was standing in the doorway, staring at you.'

'We must have got crossed lines or something.'

'I don't think you can get crossed lines with a webcam.'

I think, really think, for a moment.

'There's only me here.'

I'm not sure I've told the truth.

We finish talking, and as I close the laptop down the room feels lonely again. I'm not getting used to being on my own at all. It's strange how silence can be more bothersome than noise. The silence in this house creates a feeling of space, makes every room feel big and every hour feel like three.

My glass is empty. I pour again, and as it splashes I hear a floorboard creak overhead. I slowly look towards the ceiling.

The loft.

I walk to the landing, slowly and gently, but the floorboards still creak. All the lights are on from my earlier search. I open the door to the little narrow staircase, and when I switch the light on there, I see my hand trembling. I panic, run up the stairs. They bang beneath my feet. There's nothing here but furniture and boxes. I check behind everything, get on my hands and knees and look under everything, but there's nothing, no one. I stand at the tiny window. There are a few lights from houses on the other side of the heath and, distantly to the right, lights from cars on the main road, streaming through the dark. I see my reflection. I'm ugly.

Even though there's no one here, I still don't feel comfortable.

Back downstairs, I check all of my rooms again. Then I go down to the first floor and check all of the rooms there too. Empty. Except the locked room, which has no light showing under the door.

I stand in the hallway. This feels like Mrs Moore's part of the house and I don't think I should go into the rooms here. They must have her belongings in them.

Halfway back up the stairs, I stop. The front and back doors. I want to check if they're locked. Walking towards the back door, I feel uneasy to think that through its window I can't possibly see anyone in the darkness of the garden, but that someone could be watching me because of the light inside.

It's locked.

I walk along the hall to the front door, my heart pounding again. The chain is across it. I pull on the handle and the door doesn't budge. I push the bolt across at the bottom and the top anyway.

'You're afraid.'

I gasp and turn quickly. Mrs Moore is in the hallway, poking the fire, which I hadn't even noticed was lit. I must have walked straight past her. How did I not see her?

'I don't know what you mean.'

'You're afraid of something.' She puts a hand on her hip and bends down slowly, picks a log from the stack and gently throws it into the fire. It sends out a burst of sparks from its flames.

'I'm fine. I just wanted to check that the doors are locked.'

'I'm sure everything is going to be fine, now that you're here.' She brushes her hands clean.

'What do you mean, *now that I'm here*?'

She turns and limps to the door of her basement flat.

I lie in bed with the light on, eyes wide open. I hate this feeling, lying in bed and feeling lost, like no day has really happened, so that the night ahead feels endless, the morning impossible.

She's mad, but she's right. I am afraid. I'm afraid of myself, of what I'm doing. Running away from everything I've ever wanted, worked for, dreamed of. Mia's gone and I'm afraid. I've lost everything for love, can't go back to my life because of love, and now I'm not even sure what love is. I shut my eyes, tightly, aching for sleep to take me away.

I wake suddenly. I've slept well, much better than I have for a while. Though I lie still, I feel a little more strength than I have for a while too. I think I feel better. Its full morning and the day's early brightness bursts through the gap in the curtains. The blackbird is on his branch, singing louder than ever, every note clean and perfect.

I have a runny nose. I sniff, but it's still there so I sniff again, harder. I wipe across my face. There's a smear of red over the back of my hand now. I sit up, confused, then I see dark red dry patches all over the white pillow.

In the bathroom, I look closely in the mirror above the sink, at the blood across my face. Some of it is fresh and wet, some dried and crusted. A couple of flaky dark lines run down my neck past my ear. I turn on the tap, and without waiting for the warm water to come through, I splash my face. The icy water takes the air out of me and makes me gasp. It runs down my T-shirt and over my chest, trickles down my arms and makes me shiver. I hold my breath and splash again, again, rub hard with my fingertips against the dried streams and patches.

I look at my dripping face. All of the blood has washed away. I feel clean but I am pale and the strength I felt earlier from a restful night's sleep has gone and I shiver more. I know I must stop drinking so much, but I don't know if I can anymore. I feel its effects, good and bad, at different times of the day. Alcohol is constantly in my body. I even want a drink now.

I cup my hands under the flow of water. It's beginning to warm now. I splash my face, even though there's no blood left and my nose has stopped bleeding. I splash again, again. My hand slaps my face as regularly as the tick of a clock. I need water. I need to wash everything away.

THIRTY

We spent our honeymoon on a Mediterranean island, walking, talking, relaxing and becoming more a part of each other every day.

We came across views that were breathtaking. Winding coastline paths along sea as blue as kingfishers, with little white boats scattered everywhere. We browsed shops, bought things for the house and for people at home and sent postcards to our parents and Carl. We sat outside cafés and bars, sometimes hardly talking, just watching the sun setting over the sea at the end of long days. The peace was wonderful. Carl had said he would stay at our house while we were away so we didn't have anything to worry about at home. It felt, for that fortnight, that nowhere else existed other than that island. Even the birdsong sounded unique there. The sun looked different.

I'd never been able to keep my hands from Mia for long, but on our honeymoon I couldn't leave her alone at all. No embrace was long enough. Did she know how much she had taken over me? She told me that she did and that she felt the same about me, though I did wonder, with the feeling of love so overwhelming, so unreservedly consuming, whether it was possible that she could have the same feeling that I did.

It was like we were in a very restful place, personally. We'd both found our *one*, made our lifelong commitment in front of God and every person close to us in the world, and it felt like now we could take a huge sigh of relief. There was a profusion of calm between us and we basked in it.

In those fourteen days I became even more attached to Mia than I ever had before, and I observed her more closely. I would wake up in the morning and watch her sleeping face. It was so peaceful and full of love, even as she slept. Sometimes I'd wake in the morning and find her watching me too, stroking my hair as soon as I opened my eyes. There were times on our honeymoon, and thereafter, that I loved her so much that I really couldn't speak the words to her, the use of words not enough, gestures too awkward. I was so conscious of time, of how long we both might live, how long forever would be. It was a discovery for me, the influence one person can have over another. The power someone else's harmless body can have. I didn't even recognise myself anymore. It was just her.

People talk of love at first sight, but it wasn't like that. Though I was captivated from my first glimpse of her in the corridor at college and felt an unbearable physical attraction to her, I don't think that something as enormous as love can happen instantly. It was a gradual and continual thing, but on our honeymoon it found its home and my feelings towards Mia and her feelings towards me changed irreversibly. Things would never be the same again. When we walked up the steps to the plane to return home, I looked forward to the rest of my life so much. It was a future I could see, a guaranteed one that I could rely on, plan around, and live and be happy about.

Even after our honeymoon this feeling continued. I found myself noticing others more, other couples, other people on their own, looking a little lost. I saw a guy on a train one day and I noticed something in him. We made eye contact a couple of times. It was something I've never recognised in a stranger before. I could tell, I *knew*, that he was in love with someone, somewhere.

Mia and I rowed, of course, and so did Carl and I. Always insignificantly. The two of them never did, though sometimes they'd annoy each other and just exchange a look or a word or two. Carl would tap his teeth with his little fingernail when he was watching TV and bored and it would annoy the hell out of Mia. Sometimes he did this just to wind her up, and he'd give me a wink after she said something to him about it. She'd tut and shake her head towards the TV and he'd wink at me and then I'd get a comment from Mia too if I hadn't managed to keep my giggle silent. She'd tell us we were like a pair of kids.

I knew other couples rowed. I'd see them in the street, outside pubs, hear the neighbours through the walls. People screaming the most horrendous things at each other, objects going flying through the air with yelled words of hate, which were probably not even meant. Such violence, before a slap or a punch has even been dealt. I find even the screaming and the words to be violent when they're conveyed in that way. Mia felt the same, so those kinds of rows, which others had, we never did.

One day, it was winter, maybe two or three years after our wedding, I saw something that made my world stop.

Mia, Carl and I were in our local pub. I'd been away visiting my parents for a weekend, and following that we hadn't seen Carl for a week. I had been looking forward to catching up. We sat at our usual table and Carl was just going to buy our drinks. He knew what I'd want as we always drank the same beer, but Mia often changed hers. He stood next to her, asked her what she wanted and put his hand on her shoulder as he did so. I wouldn't have given it a second thought, but as she said that she wanted white wine she put her hand on his, on her shoulder, then very suddenly snatched it back, like she'd burnt herself. Then there was a glance, so fleeting I really had to try hard to think about whether I had seen it at all, where they looked each other in the eye, with some kind of recognition.

Something I wasn't involved in.

When Carl returned with our drinks, we all sat in a rare, uncomfortable silence.

THIRTY-ONE

I'm on the bench beside the pond with my phone in my hand, and I need to make a decision. Carl has called three times while I've been sitting here. I haven't answered, like all the other times either he or Mia have called since I got my new phone after arriving in Blackheath. They've done so at least once a day. Next time, I might answer. I'm not sure if I feel weak or strong for it. I think I'm daring myself.

Winter is here. The branches are almost stripped bare now. The grass on the heath hasn't grown for weeks. I'm wearing a jacket I found in the loft, but I need to buy a winter coat. My hands and feet are cold, but I enjoy sitting here. I like to get out of the house. The hours pass too slowly there.

My phone rings and vibrates in my hand.

Carl.

I don't know what I would say to him. What could he say to me? I can't think of any words to make sense of what happened, or where we both are in our lives now. It's all gone. There's nothing to say. I breathe deeply, until the ringing and vibrating stops.

I look across the pond at the tops of the leafless trees and, behind them, the church steeple. There's a wonderful feeling of peace here. I remember the day Parker sat beside me on this bench and how I felt that the solitude I was so comfortable in was being taken away. How I'd felt intimidated by his confidence. Now I'm pleased when I see him. I wish he was sitting beside me now.

My phone rings again.

'Hi, Carl.'

'Lewis.'

There's relief in his voice and he sighs. I can hear him breathing. He doesn't know what to say.

I watch the still water on the pond.

After all the years of friendship, all the experiences, the conversations, the things that only we knew, it's all been replaced with what I saw that morning, which I saw for only a few seconds, but which I've imagined so many times since. Everything fell apart that quickly after I saw them together that morning.

'Are you OK?'

I don't know what he means, whether I am OK right now in this moment, or in my life now. I don't know if he feels the distance between us, as I do, a distance so vast that it's too personal for me to tell him how I am and too intrusive for him to ask.

'Where are you?'

'I don't want to tell you where I am.'

'That's OK, really it's OK. I'm just pleased you picked up your phone.'

'I wasn't going to.' I feel that I'm being rude, or unreasonable. Why am I being so unreasonable?

Silence again, this time broken by a pair of parakeets that pass, screeching, over the heath. They perch amongst the treetops behind the pond.

'Is Mia OK?'

I regret the words immediately, but I do want to know

how she is. I've wanted to know since I left her, but me asking Carl about Mia feels wrong. It's the wrong way around.

'I think she's fine.'

My mind leaps onto the word *think* and what it could mean. Maybe he doesn't know because he hasn't seen her. Maybe she's beside him right now and a vague answer to my question was an easy one. All the questions I've been trying to keep from my mind, I want to know the answers now. I want to know what has been happening. I don't even know how many weeks it's been since I crashed my car and then saw them together. There are lost weeks, weeks where, for the first time, I have no idea what Mia and Carl have been doing. I even want to ask if he's OK. I won't.

'Have you got somewhere to live?'

'Yes, and a job, so don't worry about me.'

Even though the circumstances couldn't be worse, I feel a little satisfaction at telling him of my independence. I didn't even realise I had it until now.

'Good. I've been so worried. Lewis, I'm so sorry for everything that's happened.'

I don't know what to say to him. No words can tell him about the loss I feel. No apologies can make up for it. I don't say anything. I just watch the parakeets in the tops of the trees, scratching their beaks against the branches.

'Lewis, we need to meet.'

THIRTY-TWO

Life settled, seasons passed, and the three of us lived through the days of our adult lives in London.

Sometimes I still felt a little old before my time when I saw other people our age. They were having fun and seemingly loving their life, but I realised something in the end. Most of them were out having all this fun, meeting new people, because they were looking for what I had already found. What I'd been fortunate enough to find so early on in life. Being settled, having a home. Finding the person I love and who loves me. A long-lasting, solid friendship. I had the things that everyone dreams of and I was aware of them. I was grateful for them every day.

Mia was happy too. She had hobbies, mostly involving the garden and the house. She put a lot of effort into us having a good home. In the garden, she looked after the trees, shrubs and flowers. So many flowers. A lawn without a weed, just like Dad would keep ours back home in Whiteflower. She worked full-time in the florists she had worked in at the weekends when she was at university. Her plans of a career in fashion had been put on hold. She often told me how happy she was, though she really didn't need to say. I could see it. I've always thought that people who are truly happy have a unique kind of beauty, and I could see it in Mia every day.

Sometimes I thought Carl was happy too. He had continued to do well in his career and still rented the same flat in Leytonstone. He began to get on better with his dad, and in the end his dad was proud of what Carl had achieved, as mine was of me. Carl was still single as he, the last of the three of us, reached his thirtieth birthday. In the years since Mia and I had got married, Carl had a few one-night stands, few enough to count on one hand, and not one girlfriend. He told me in detail about the one-night stands and, in a purely physical way, I did envy his freedom to experience such things, just a little, though I never wanted to be without my marriage as I knew the feeling of happiness that came with it. I felt sorry for Carl, that he didn't have the same feeling in his life, that his only glimpses of intimacy or love were from the touch of a stranger, then snatched suddenly back. I felt even more sorry for him that he didn't appear to mind that.

He was, I was sure of it, still a man with something on his mind, and in all those years he'd never told me what it was. As the years wore on, the look of defeat in his expression appeared more and more like he was being worn down, ageing too soon, from the inside out.

The year we all turned thirty had been the hottest summer I had ever known. It was sweltering. Every day was filled with the most excessive heat. In the streets, strangers looked at each other with a rare glance of recognition as they wiped the back of their hand over their brow or stopped to drink from bottled water, which everyone was advising everyone else to do. Sparrows and thrushes, the most frequent visitors to our garden, sat on the fence with their thirsty beaks gaping and we left saucers of water on the grass for them. Pigeons, instead of flapping around in search of food or chasing each other, relaxed contemplatively in the shade with their wings spread flat on the ground.

Mia, Carl and I enjoyed weekends in the garden and the park, eating ice creams, ice lollies and drinking ice-cold drinks. We read books and walked around barefoot. Every weekend, it felt like we were on holiday.

One day that summer, the three of us spent a day in the garden along with the neighbours from either side of our house. Two couples, one in their twenties and the other in their seventies. We always got along well. Mia and I had prepared food for most of the morning before their arrival. Carl even made some of the food, putting random selections of things on cocktail sticks. Cucumber with cheese, ham with tofu dipped in soy sauce. The neighbours brought wine and beer with them.

Towards late evening, both sets of neighbours left at the same time. We saw them out and the three of us returned to the garden, to our chairs and blanket on the grass. It was just starting to get dark. A magnificent orange sun was spread across the sky. We chatted and laughed and told each other jokes, though Mia could never remember hers properly, which made me and Carl laugh before she'd finished them, and she told us both to shut up and listen. As the last of the light seeped from the sky, I dozed on the blanket on the grass and fell into a wonderfully peaceful sleep. Sleeping outside always made me think of Whiteflower Woods and the miles of countryside that we had claimed as our own. I've always felt a sense of belonging with nature.

When I woke, alone in the dark, there were still plates, bottles and glasses, everything everywhere. I'd not been asleep for long, I didn't think. The outside light was on, which gave a little light over the patio area, which I then walked over, towards the door. I could see into the living room through the kitchen window. There was movement there, Mia and Carl. My eyes froze on Carl.

He was doing up the thin black leather belt on top of the

cut-off blue denim jeans he'd been wearing all day. Mia was lounging on the sofa.

I walked into the house.

'Hi, Lewis,' she said, so casually that it took away from what Carl was still doing.

Doing up his belt.

I just stood there. Carl sat in the armchair and Mia remained on the sofa. We all just looked at one another and I couldn't utter a word.

THIRTY-THREE

Jessica is sitting opposite me, examining the wine list for an exceptionally long time. I wish she'd hurry up as I really need a drink. A beer or a whisky. Anything.

We've been to see a film tonight. Horror, her choice. She'd told me before that it was her favourite genre, that no other type of film has the same impact on her. I went along with whatever she wanted to see, though I'm not sure I'll do it again. It was a horrendous tale of violence and terror, though I must admit that every time it made me jump it also made me laugh.

Jessica was excited by the film, looked at me after scary moments and covered her face with her hands, though I think she still looked through gaps in her fingers. At one particularly shocking moment, she gripped the sides of her chair. I found her more entertaining than the film. She kept offering me some of her drink and I drank from her straw. It felt strange to do that, but not enough to put me off from doing it. She ate sweets throughout the film and I smelled cola and lemon and sherbet on her breath in the near darkness.

We're in a bar in Canary Wharf. Finally, I have a beer and she has a white wine, having made her big decision. We've ordered food and Jessica already has her knife and fork in position each side of where her plate will be placed. I take my cutlery from the napkin and do the same, though I don't know why as I wouldn't normally do this. In the middle of the table, a tiny vase with a single pink flower sits between us.

To others, we probably look like a couple, or two people out on a date. She's pretty. I think most men would want to sleep with her at the end of the night if they were in my position. I don't know why I don't have these feelings. Well, I do have them, I just don't seem to have any drive to do anything about them. As Mia is the only woman I've ever slept with, I can only associate it with her. The idea of sleeping with anyone else is just fantasy. Now that I have the option of doing so, it feels odd. It's an exciting thought at times, but I'm not sure I really like the idea. It mostly feels wrong, my desires a burden. Spending time with Jessica is beginning to feel nice though. We're becoming friends. A female friend is rare for me. There have been the work colleagues on the team I managed, which seems such a distant world now, even though it was only a couple of months ago. They were exactly that, though, work colleagues. There was Carl's older sister, Kelly, too, who was a friend of a kind, though we didn't always get on and I've not seen her since my wedding. Aunt Ruth, even though a relative, was definitely a friend. I can't believe it's been nearly twenty years since she died. I think that even if I live to be an old man, I'll never completely understand her death.

Jessica has said something, but I'm not sure what. She's smiling at me.

'You're daydreaming again, Lewis.'

I laugh. It feels so good to be in her company, but a fleeting feeling of dread comes over me now as I think our time together has to end later and I have to go back to number 28, with its coldness and loneliness and empty rooms. I keep hoping a room will become available in Jessica and Eugene's house and that they'll suggest I move in, but neither of them has said anything about it.

Our food arrives.

'What's up?' She digs into her spaghetti.

I look down at the burger on my plate but my appetite has gone and my headache is back. I need another beer.

'There's something weird about that house.'

'What house?'

'The house I live in.'

'Apart from the fact that it looks like no one's lived there for years?'

I think she means it as a joke, but it makes me feel uncomfortable, as I've thought the exact same thing myself when I've walked across the heath and seen its empty windows, broken chimney pots and the tree-ish thing that sprouts from the gutter.

'There's just something not right with it. It gives me the creeps sometimes.'

'Aww, don't you like the dark on your own?'

'There's either something wrong with the house or there's something wrong with me.'

I watch her laugh, but then her smile fades. She puts her fork down on her plate and looks at me awkwardly, in a way she's never done before.

THIRTY-FOUR

One October morning, I woke on the sofa.

Mia had the day off as she had some holiday to use up and was going to the garden centre. Carl also had the day off. He had stayed the night in the box room and said he would drive Mia to the garden centre before he went home.

I had a short, hot shower and then dried myself on the soft white towels that Mia always put fresh in the bathroom cupboard. I put my boxer shorts on, wiped the mist from the mirror and watched as I brushed my teeth. I'd aged in those years since I got married. Little lines had appeared beside my eyes and my skin looked tougher than when I was younger.

I continued dressing, and it took longer than usual. Then I went downstairs to the kitchen, made myself a cup of tea and sat at the breakfast bar, looking out into the garden as I drank in sips. We usually had toast in the garden in the mornings, but it was just me getting up for work that day so I decided to pick up some breakfast on the way.

I walked back upstairs and into our bedroom. I kissed Mia on the shoulder, one of the only parts of her body exposed to the cool morning air. She didn't stir.

I checked myself in the hallway mirror. Hair tidy enough, tie straight, all ready for a day at work. I got into my car and began to drive down the road. There was hardly any traffic. Rush hour was yet to begin. It felt good to be driving away from them that morning. Away from it all.

A little way from the house, I don't know what happened but my car flipped and landed on its roof.

As I sat on the kerb after, rubbing my head where it had been banged in the crash, knowing I had to get away before the police arrived, I noticed a little dog watching me from the other side of the road. He had his head tilted to one side. He looked at me with an expression of sympathy.

THIRTY-FIVE

This morning I will see Carl for the first time in weeks and weeks. It's the longest time I've ever not seen him. Though I've never thought about it before, I realise now that with the exception of my honeymoon, I've seen Carl nearly every day of my life, until I saw what I saw. Agreeing to meet up with him felt like my biggest defeat since I walked quietly from the house that morning. In the dark weeks that followed, I've realised I have no fight in me at all, which makes me feel pointless.

The short train journey to the West End is awful. I feel travel-sick. I don't suffer from travel sickness. We're meeting at a pub on the river near London Bridge, one of the places we used to go and have drunken nights together after we first moved to London. I don't know why, but when he asked where I wanted to meet, it was the first place that came into my mind.

There are things I want to know, things I feel ready to know now. I need some answers about what's happened, before I meet with Mia. I think he was surprised that I agreed to meet with him before her. Even through his betrayal, I want to talk to him about things first. It feels like the most natural thing to do. It makes me feel defeated again to realise this.

I arrive at the pub, its familiarity hitting me unexpectedly. I spot the tables we'd sat at on our many visits here, each with a different memory attached to them. The fireplace roars welcome, but it's not as cold today. I breathe in the warm stench of beer, so good it makes my eyes close for a moment. When they open, I notice that all the tables have people sitting at them. I hear the constant rumble of chatter. Carl's not here.

I walk through the bar and into the garden. He's sitting with his back to me, leans his elbows on the table, on which are two pints, untouched. I watch him. He's wearing the same black jacket he's had for years, the one he always brings out in winter. He rubs his hand on his forehead a few times, and then slowly, as if hearing a sound that I know I haven't made, he turns around in small, jarred movements.

His hair is shorter than normal. Spikier. It makes his face look fresh. I notice the shape of his face now too, the strength of his cheekbones, the flawlessness of his skin and the influence of his blue eyes. How did I ever think that Mia hadn't noticed him in that way before? As I walk closer, his expression drops. He looks shocked to see me, as if we haven't arranged to meet.

'Lewis,' he says. He stands and holds out his hand for me to shake. 'Oh God, Lewis, you don't look well.'

His hand. So familiar. Slightly darker skin than his face. A wide silver ring on his thumb. Fingers chubby for his build. I look at his hand but I can't touch it. He lowers it, slowly, then sits again.

I sit too. There's a couple at a table at the other end of the garden, and in the sky over the river seagulls are circling around and around. In the centre of the table, bottles of sauce stand huddled, dried bits crusted around their lids.

I know I have to look at him but I don't want to. I can't.

The wooden table has indecipherable words scratched squarely into it. I tilt my head slightly and squint, but I still can't make them out. Grains of salt are scattered in and around them. A pigeon walks between and under the tables, picking at things on the ground that I can't see, purple shimmering on its neck.

I don't know what Carl sees when he looks at me now, but he looks sad. Like he could cry, but I know he won't, not in front of anyone. When I look at him now I feel jealous. I feel not good enough.

'I'm so sorry, Lewis.'

Carl would have been the first, probably only person I'd have talked to about this situation if it had been a different man I'd found with Mia. He'd have known the right words to say to give me some peace, know the right advice to give to help me see things clearly. He'd have helped me make decisions for myself.

'I'd really like to explain what happened.' He looks at me, right in the eyes.

'OK.' I don't know what to say. I feel too proud to ask him my questions now and I feel foolish for it. Maybe letting him speak will be the easiest way to take this.

He looks to the sky for a moment. 'I completely had in mind what I was going to say to you today, but it's all gone.' His voice is dry. 'I'm sorry, is what I want to say more than anything.'

'You've already said that.'

'But I don't feel I can say it enough.' He looks almost panicked.

'Tell me what you had ready to say.' I take a few deep breaths, remain calm. I'm going to have to listen to this. I wanted to hear it, after all. That's the reason I agreed to us meeting. There's no point in backing out now.

'Well, I feel the same way about her that you do.'

'No you don't,' I snap. 'You can't.' I turn and look at the City across the river. The view has become hazy. It's going to rain. I try to just think of the rain.

'The morning I found you both, was that the only time you slept with her?'

'No.'

I feel the first spits of rain on my face. Tiny cold needles piercing my skin.

'You knew, didn't you?'

I can't answer him. I can't say the word.

'You were drinking all the time, Lewis. Your marriage was a wreck. She wasn't going to put up with that, she's too level-headed. You knew that.'

'Oh, so you had to step in and help. I'll fucking thank you for that then, shall I?'

'I didn't mean it like that. But you ruined things for yourself. You were even pissed that morning you crashed your car. I found the bottle in the bin.'

'I can't remember.'

'Well that's convenient for you. I don't even know why you were trying to go to work anyway, you knew full well they'd sacked you for missing too many days.'

The rain is beginning to fall properly now. The temperature is still mild though. Freezing weather will be here soon. Frosts and ice. The silence and death of everything. Carl is speaking again.

'…is there? There's something not right. You don't look well.'

I don't care. 'I have some stuff I want to ask you. Please be honest with me.'

'Of course I will,' he says, looking confused, as if he'd never tell me a lie. A couple of months ago, I would never have needed to ask for his honesty.

'How many times did you sleep with her?'

His eyes close slightly, then open again, and for a moment nothing is said. He's not having to recall anything, he's just trying to find words. I'm recognising more in him now than I ever realised I knew.

'I have no idea.'

The blood is draining from me. I think I might have heard enough. My face is going numb. My mind floods. I want to come back at Carl with proof that all this can't have happened, but I can't.

I knew.

We hold eye contact for a while, until I can't look at him any longer and my eyes close suddenly, as if I've been in a dark room and someone has just turned the light on. When they open again, I'm looking at the square scratched letters on the table.

'How many times?'

'I don't know.'

'How many?' I'm angry now.

He shakes his head from side to side, slowly. 'I don't know,' he says. Then he looks towards the river, deep in thought for a moment. Then back at me, right in the eye. His eyes are full of tears, but they won't flow. 'Every time I went to her. Lewis, I love her.'

I hadn't been ready to hear this. Hearing that it was just sex, that he might lie and try to tell me it had only happened that once, try to dismiss it as a casual thing, I was prepared for, but not this. Why won't he lie to me?

My hand reaches out and hits the left side of his face, near his nose. He gasps and jumps up, holds his hand to the place where I've just hit.

The man and woman stand at their table at the other end of the garden, looking at me, disgusted. They sit back down but don't speak to each other and watch us like they're watching television.

Carl holds his hand on his face, though it can't hurt. He shows no retaliation. He's not scared of me. He sits again.

'So you slept with her loads of times.'

'Yes.'

I try to imagine how it happened the first time, how one of them first touched the other. Who touched first? How the touch of friendship could change into something different. I try to imagine how they did it. I want to know where. Was it always in my bed? I want to know every detail. I want to know if he liked it and if she liked it, whether she gripped the back of his hair and whispered into his ears the words she did in mine.

'I'm so sorry, Lewis.'

My hand, crunched into a fist now, lands neatly on the side of his face.

The man rushes over. 'Now pack it in you,' he says.

I stand. He's about a foot shorter than me and tough-looking. The woman comes to his side, looking nervous.

'You need to piss off, mate,' I say, pointing my finger an inch from his face. I don't care if he fucking kills me.

The woman tugs at his arm. 'Just leave it,' she says. 'It's not our business.' She tugs until he walks away. They don't go back to their table but leave the garden, looking back until they're out of sight.

I turn to Carl. His trembling hand is resting on his face, a line of blood over his fingers and chin. He's not fighting back and I know I'm in control now. It makes me want to carry on, to defeat him completely. His tears are on the brink of flowing. A part of me wants to see him break, so I don't say anything. I watch.

'I know you hate me for this, but it wasn't always one-sided, you know. She wanted it too. But I know if I hadn't have pushed, none of this would have happened. I take all the blame. Will you try to sort things out with Mia?' His voice is desperate.

I don't like the way he speaks about her with such familiarity. I've always liked it before, but now it feels too close. I don't want to answer his question. I just want to watch.

'She's shattered, I'm shattered, but that's my problem. I don't want you to lose everything because of me, Lewis. What's important is you and Mia. The two of you have always been the most important thing to me, you know that. That hasn't changed.'

But everything's changed.

Everything's been taken. It feels like I never had it, like it was all make-believe. My marriage, our love. My friendship with Carl, like it has never existed.

'If I could change it I would, but I can't. I'll never forgive myself. So go on,' he says, arms out at his sides, bloody palms turned upwards. 'Hit me again.' He screams. 'Fucking hit me.'

THIRTY-SIX

I knock on the door of Jessica and Eugene's house, take a step back and look up. Their bedroom lights are on. Jessica has invited me around. It's Sunday, so the restaurant is closed. She said that Eugene will be home too, as a date has cancelled on him at the very last minute. She texted me this information with an *lol* at the end of it.

She opens the door, smiles, reaches out and puts her hand around the back of my head to get a firm grip, and then plants a kiss on my cheek. I take off my new coat, scarf and gloves in the hallway, and leave them on the hooks on the wall. The house is warm. Jessica wears blue denim jeans, well fitted I notice, as she walks up the stairs in front of me, and a tight T-shirt. I know Eugene will make a comment to me about it all at some point when she's not in the room, or maybe when she is.

When we reach her bedroom, Eugene is ripping open a box of beers.

'Leeewis!' he says, with a big smile, and he reaches his hand to shake mine, which he always does when he sees me.

I wince when he shakes it. I pull my hand back and we

both look down.

'Wow, what have you been up to?' he says, holding me delicately by the fingertips.

I see Carl on the floor in the beer garden, struggling to get up, coughing and choking, blood dripping from his mouth onto the ground.

My knuckles are swollen, red, purple and cut. The back of my hand feels like air is being pumped into it every few seconds. I held it under the cold tap for ages last night and this morning, but it's still swollen.

Jessica has taken my hand from Eugene and she's holding me by the wrist. I wish I hadn't come here now.

'I banged it on something last night.'

Jessica looks at me doubtfully, but I know her well enough that she will ask nothing further for now.

'Were you pissed *again*?' Eugene asks.

'I don't drink that much.'

He raises his eyebrows. 'I thought I drank a lot until I met you.'

Jessica has given my hand back and is changing the subject for me.

'We're having pizza again.'

We're in Jessica's bedroom. I'm in the armchair, she's on her bed and Eugene lies on the floor as he talks and watches the film intermittently. She has chosen a horror film for us. The last slices of pizza, garlic bread and bits of salad in plastic tubs lie around us. We're picking them up every now and then but are complaining that we're too full. I'm wondering if they ever cook, or if delivered pizza is the norm here.

They're very casual with each other, even with me. I can't help but compare them to Mia and Carl and the three of us spending time together on the countless nights in we've shared since our teenage years. Jessica and Eugene treat me as they do each other, but I do feel that they are the two together here, and that I'm the visitor. With Mia and

Carl, I was the one that brought them together. I was the solid thing in the middle. Essential. At least, I thought I was. I wonder if she's nursing his wounds.

The lead actress in the film is running through her house being chased by a murderer when she should be running out of the door. Eugene grips his head and yells at the TV.

'You *stupid* cow!'

Jessica laughs.

Eugene doesn't take his eyes from the screen.

'Do you think she's beautiful?' Jessica looks at Eugene, but as he doesn't answer she looks at me instead.

I look at the TV. 'Yes, she's quite pretty.'

'I think she is too,' she says.

'I'd definitely do her,' Eugene adds, still looking at the screen, though he has taken his hands from his head to reach for a slice of pizza.

I look to Jessica, expecting a reaction to what Eugene has just said, but she just looks at him for a moment and then back to the TV. I want her to say something to him. My face is burning and my heart speeding up. I look at Eugene, who is lost within the film, and I hate him for his want and need to *do* people, for his ability to do them without caring. I take quiet, deep breaths.

'I'm just going to the toilet,' I say, but neither of them look up.

In the bathroom, I turn on the taps and splash water over my face. I look in the mirror, at the drops of water on my cheeks and chin. 'You're an idiot,' I whisper, looking directly into my eyes. They're the same green as Parker's. I realise now that I haven't seen him around for a week or two.

In Jessica's bedroom, they're both sitting in the same positions as when I left the room.

The conversations they have together, the things he says in front of her, still shock me at times. The actress in the film, who has now left her house and is being chased through a field in darkness, if Carl had said that about her in front of Mia, she would have told him to have some respect or something, but Carl would never have said that in front of Mia.

We've had a lot to drink. Jessica has fallen asleep on her bed. I'm feeling tipsy, thankfully. After seeing Carl yesterday, I had whisky when I got home and I've been feeling ill all day. The food tonight has helped though.

There are sounds here, not loud, but noticeable. Maybe I notice them more due to the silence of the house I live in. In this house, I hear toilets flushing and doors slamming on the other floors. From downstairs, a woman laughs out loud every now and then. A little while ago, a girl and a guy – a couple Eugene told me after they'd left – popped up to say hi. I like this communal house and realise the loneliness of my own again. There, I occasionally hear the front door close, or Mrs Moore stoking a fire somewhere in the house, the sound travelling up through the chimneys and past my walls on their way to the chimney tops. Sometimes, at night, I still hear her walking around the house, speaking quietly to God.

Jessica is still asleep. Eugene has said he will throw a blanket over her. He walks downstairs with me. It's a cold night and I stand by the front door, pulling on my coat and scarf and gloves. He looks at my hand again as I put my gloves on.

'Does it hurt?'

'A little. It's fine though.'

He opens the door to let me out.

'I hope everything's OK, mate,' he says. 'You know you only have to say if you ever need anything.'

'Thank you.'

'See you tomorrow,' he says. Then he puts his arm around me and hugs me tightly, just for a second. It feels good. It's such an unfamiliar gesture from him. I know for sure he knows something is wrong now. It feels good that he knows.

'Goodnight, mate.'

I step out, into the black night.

THIRTY-SEVEN

I arrive at St James's Park and look across the lake. Patches of ice lie on its surface and a moorhen walks delicately over one. I don't look towards the meeting place. I don't want to see her from a distance. I think that if I do, I might not be able to walk to her.

My footsteps crunch on the gravel path. The shining sun glitters on the stones. I hear music, laughter, summer sounds from a crowd of young people who stand near the lake in gloves and hats and scarves. Winter pansies fill the flowerbeds. People pass by me. It's happiness I see, as I walk along the path towards the lake, where Mia and I would feed the ducks when we used to come here.

When I reach the lake, I look up and see her. She's sitting a little way along the bank, on a bench near the bridge, our agreed meeting place. She's wearing a long fluffy white coat, black boots and a blue woollen hat, which must be new. Her dark straight hair shines on her shoulders. Her bag sits on her lap. She clutches it with both hands.

I've not seen her eyes yet. I can't even see her face properly, but the way she holds herself has changed. She doesn't look like the Mia of my mind. She sits like an old person. I begin to shake when I think that her frailty might be due to me leaving her, worrying her. Giving up on her.

I watch her, thinking about the times we've had together and what has brought us here, to meet in a park as I can't even bear to go to our home. She was my everything. Is my everything. She's the reason I loved life. I see her hair now and think of how she twirls it around her fingertips when she's bored. How I tease her when our alarm goes off for work and she doesn't want to wake up, so I twirl her hair so it annoys her and she laughs and slaps my hand away. How she makes sure I'm drinking enough water, spends hours cooking nice meals and how much I appreciate it. How we fall asleep at night holding hands. How caring and loving she is. How her laugh makes me laugh. It's all gone. None of it's mine now. It feels like something someone else has and I don't.

I can't see it any longer.

I turn and walk back along the path, much faster than before. I want to get away before she sees me. I mustn't see her face. Her eyes. Her regret. I can't hear any more apologies.

I run and don't stop until I reach The Mall. I hail a taxi to take me back to Blackheath.

I'm in bed and the room is spinning. I look around for the bottle. It's empty, lying on its side next to the bed. Parker is sitting on the floor, his back leaning against the wall. I know he hasn't been here all night, but I vaguely remember him helping me get into bed. I think I might have been on the floor before that.

'Life is short. Don't be bitter about what you've lost.'

'But I should have spoken to her. I want her to know. I want to tell her how even if she thought about it really hard, tried to imagine it, she'd never be able to understand how much I miss her.'

'Don't cry. You need to accept that things won't feel the same as before you loved her. It's over.'

I wish he knew how wrong he is, but he's too young to know. I want to tell him what life can be like, about how I can't do this.

I try to focus on him. I can't see him properly.

I open my eyes. It's morning. The blackbird is on his branch outside the window, singing heartily.

Parker is gone.

I make tea. My throat is tight and my head hurts. I can't remember the last time I felt well. I must try to drink less, though I'll have to start tomorrow as I'm meeting Eugene tonight. In the living room I sip my tea and look over the heath. It's empty today. There's a light frost and a low mist. I see halfway across until it disappears into nothingness, like the air itself is covered with snow. The mist has been over the heath for days. It clears a little, then falls again.

I could have spoken to Mia yesterday, but I ran away. I can't believe I ran when I had my chance to talk to her, or remember why I did. My mind is as misted up as the heath.

A man is sitting on the bench on the other side of the road, at the edge of the grass. He is looking out over the white of the heath. As I watch him I begin to realise, slowly, that it's the same man, wearing the same dark coat and hat, that I've seen sitting there before. How many times, I don't know – two, three times. I have no idea how often I've seen him there, now I think about it, but I know I've seen him a lot before, sitting there on the right-hand side of the bench, his back to the house. He might have been there every time I've looked from this window and every time I've walked in and out of the house. I try to think of when I've seen him there, how many times. It might be twenty. He's always there. He has a small build. With his mac and hat, he's like a fictional detective.

Condensation gathers on the window. I want to see him

better, so I lift the window open. It sticks a couple of times, but with one firm pull, it lifts. A bitter draft covers me and rushes into the house. My breath clouds white.

In a small but sudden movement, his head turns to the side just slightly, as if he's just heard a sound. Or a whisper. Then, he is still.

I turn from the window to find my trainers. One in the bedroom and one in the kitchen. I twist into them and I run down the stairs, bang-banging on the floorboards through the quiet of the house. When I open the front door, the heath emerges before me, bigger than ever. Through the fog I can see no end to it. I walk out the door and stand at the top of the steps. Across the road, the bench is empty. I look left, then right, walk slowly across the road to the edge of the heath, but I can't see him. There's no one here at all. I stand beside the bench, turn in a full circle, twice. I wonder where he's gone, how he could have disappeared so quickly. Maybe he has a car, though I didn't hear one, but I wasn't listening. I was running down the stairs as fast as I could.

The bench is covered evenly with dew. I lean down and wipe my hand across and it showers to the ground. I sit in the clear patch I have made, on the right-hand side. Where he was. The mist is beginning to clear now. Slowly, a spectacular view begins to emerge. I can understand why he picks this spot. I wonder what he thinks as he sits here, whether he looks out, or within. There's so much to see from here. So much beauty. So much nature. I wonder what the heath would be like if it was left to grow wild. It wouldn't take long, a few summers at the most before the overgrown grass would become dotted with bushes and saplings. Weeds and bracken would eventually rule. It must have been like that sometime, before the village was built. The more the fog clears, the more there is to think about from here.

Suddenly, the mist has nearly cleared and I have no idea how long I've been sitting here. I remember now that, as the heath lies empty in front of me, the house stands high behind me. Stronger now, I feel its presence and the increasing thump in my heart changes from nervousness to panic. I feel afraid to look behind me, but as the feeling and the pounding deepens, the power from the house grows and my fear makes me turn around. I look up at the window, certain that I was being watched, but it's bare and empty, half open as I had left it.

I sigh deeply, relieved at the faceless window. I lean back on the bench. Over the wonderful emptiness of the heath, the mist starts to gather again.

THIRTY-EIGHT

We walk along the carriage until we find two empty seats, as the train rolls out of Blackheath Station. I've given in to Eugene's demands for us to have a night out and I'm annoyed at myself. I don't really want it now.

It's the first time we've been out of work by eight, as the restaurant had no bookings for tonight. It's Monday. We both went home and got changed, then had two quick drinks in a pub on the heath before walking to the station. I can feel their effects.

We sit opposite one another, each side of a window. It's dark and the view is mostly obscured by reflections from inside the train. It's surprisingly busy and most people look dressed for a night out. Eugene's aftershave scents the air. He has a kind of nervous energy tonight and bounces his heels up and down on the floor. He's excited, like a child.

We are going to meet a couple of Eugene's friends in a bar in Charing Cross and go from there. I'm not used to an evening out being so unplanned, but I go along with it. I have no choice now I've come this far. Eugene is determined to give me a good night, and in some way I don't want to disappoint him either.

As we edge into central London, the train curves between buildings and screeches as it shifts tracks. I look out at the lit City. Here, shiny new office buildings tower awkwardly between smaller, beautiful buildings with engravings on their walls, observatories and roof gardens. Their bricks are dirty and they sit like stubborn squatters as the City develops around them. I need to come for a walk around here soon. I like seeing this. Eugene has picked up a newspaper which had been left on the floor. He noisily turns the pages, too quickly to read anything more than a headline on each page. He's impatient. When nearly at the end of the paper he folds it in half, drops it back on the floor, tuts and looks at me.

'A cab home later would be quick and easy,' he says enthusiastically, like he's advertising cabs.

'You said it was too expensive.'

He rolls his eyes and then looks out of the window and points as the train crosses the river at Charing Cross. 'Tide's in.'

The river is full and turbulent, sparklingly lit from London around it. Big Ben's strong hands sit at ten twenty. I think of my journey to Blackheath starting at this point of the river only weeks ago, though it feels like years and years now. So long, that I think for a moment about whether I actually made that journey, or if it was just that someone else told me they once did it.

'Has it really only been a few weeks?'

'What the fuck are you talking about, Patrick?'

I shudder, go cold in a second. 'What did you just call me?'

'Huh?'

'Why did you call me Patrick?'

'What? I called you Lewis. That is your name, isn't it, pisshead?' Eugene looks at me, confused, then shakes his head a few times. 'Two pints and you're on your way already.

You're a cheap date.' He leans forward and slaps his hands on my knees as the train comes to a stop. 'Let's go.'

The pub is busy, though not packed. It's a traditional-looking place, but it's fake traditional for tourists. A better venue than I'd have guessed Eugene would have picked when he described it as a bar, so I feel happy and a little relieved. We wait to be served.

'So, when was the last time you went clubbing, Lewis?' Eugene leans against the bar as he speaks. His confidence is infectious. I lean too.

'To be honest, I've never actually been clubbing. Been to lots of pubs, but not a club.'

'You being serious?'

'Yeah. We'd go to pubs, or see a show or a film.'

'You and your wife, you mean?'

'Yeah.' I meant Carl too.

'You married types are well boring,' he says, looking disappointed.

'I've just always thought of clubs as a place where people go to pull.'

'Yep, pretty much right,' he says, though I think he's joking. 'And you look all set for it. Is this new?'

He straightens the collar on my shirt.

'Yeah. I'm not on the pull though.'

'Oh yes you are,' Eugene says, laughing.

I manage to laugh with him.

I go to the toilets. Not because I need to, but just to have a moment. I look in the mirror. I do actually look a bit better tonight. He's pulled my collar up straight though. I fold it back down. When I return to the bar and to Eugene, there are two women standing with him.

'Lewis!' Eugene is acting suspiciously pleased to see me. He has his arm around one of the women, who has bushy, curly brown hair like a teenager from an eighties' film. She kisses him on the cheek as I walk over to them. 'This is

Shelly.' He points to her and she kisses a couple more times. Then, he turns to the other, more attractive but uncomfortable-looking woman. 'Diane, *this* is Lewis.' He's clearly been telling her about me, and as he puts his arm behind her and pushes her forward just a little, he shines a satisfied smile at me.

There's one for him and one for me. I can't believe I didn't see this coming. I'd do anything to make this moment end right now and to be on my own with Eugene, so I can tell him what a dick he is.

'Lewis, this is Diane.'

'Hello.'

'Hi.'

Diane looks shy. God knows what I look like. We shake hands awkwardly. My joints have suddenly become stiff and I'm not sure if I'm crushing her hand or shaking it gently like an old person might, but she pulls away quickly. Luckily, Eugene breaks the moment by asking them what they would both like to drink, asking me to buy them and telling us all that we only have fifteen minutes to drink up and get to the club before the entry price doubles at eleven.

The club has been packed all night. There are groups, couples and people on their own. The dance floor is a mass of bobbing shoulders and heads with the occasional arm and hand waving in the air. The dancers overflow to the stairs, between tables and in front of the bar. There are lights everywhere, swirling around madly as lasers cut through smoke. The music is the loudest I've ever heard. The sound is of a quality I've never heard before either. Its beat bursts through the room twice a second and vibrates through my trainers, which stick to the tacky floor with each step. I'm enjoying myself much more than I expected.

Eugene and Shelly have been gone for quite some time and I suspect they may be doing something in a dark corner. I stand on the balcony, which forms a complete circle above the massive dance floor. Diane has gone to get us a drink and I've stayed to keep our little spot. It's packed here too, though we've managed to have some conversation together over the music. It doesn't sound like the song has changed in the hours we've been here, but only varied, changed in pace from fast to very fast, then back to fast again.

I'm beginning to tire of the night and hope that the journey home might begin soon. We're getting a cab no matter what Eugene wants now. The first trains of the day must be starting, but I can't imagine getting on one with commuters after all the drinks I've had during the night.

It's been a different experience here to what I expected. I expected rough people, maybe a fight or two, but instead there's a unified atmosphere of fun and enjoyment. There's an unexpected level of intimacy in the crowds, too, as there's hardly any space to move. Where you want to step, there will already be someone else's foot. People put their hands on each other's waists or shoulders as they pass, for balance. Personal space doesn't exist here and no one seems to mind.

Along the balcony opposite I see people kiss, people dance, and a guy, his elbows leaning casually on the railing, looking down at the dance floor. Through the smoke and lights it takes me a moment to register his familiarity, but then I'm stunned to realise that it's Parker. I've only ever seen him in Blackheath. I'd never have imagined he'd come to a place like this. As usual, he's wearing that jacket of his, probably the only person here wearing one. I wonder where he's left Stamp. I've never seen him without that dog. His gaze is directed down to the dance floor. Concentrating. Something has got his attention and he's observing closely. I look down to where he looks and see Eugene. He's dancing freely, his arms half raised, a bottle of something in one hand. He's lost in enjoyment. I look back up at Parker. He's not taken his eyes off Eugene. He's transfixed.

'Sorry I was gone for so long.' Diane is suddenly next to me, offering a plastic cup of whisky. 'There was a queue at the bar.'

'Be back in a minute,' I say loudly towards her ear, over the music. 'I've just seen a friend. I won't be long.'

She nods and smiles.

I struggle around the balcony, through the crowds. There seems even less space now. People haven't even begun to go home yet. While trying to pass between a group of people, I lose my footing, put an arm on a shoulder for balance as I fall backwards, then out of nowhere a hand comes through the crowd and pulls me back up. I say *thank you*, but in the crowd, no one is looking at me. I don't even know if it was a man or a woman.

I reach the place on the balcony where Parker was, but I can't find him. I'm definitely in the right place, as the couple I'd seen from the other side of the balcony are kissing beside me, but I can't see Parker anywhere. There's a little empty space at the railing where he was and I stand in it. I see Diane opposite, dancing gently. She's OK. I lean on the railing and see Eugene on the dance floor. His arms are raised, body swaying, his feet stamping around, but then he stops and very suddenly he's not moving at all, like someone's switched him off. For a moment he stands motionless and I watch him closely, wondering what's wrong with him. Then, in one slow movement he turns and looks up at me, straight in the eyes, as if he knew I was here, watching him. He looks concerned, or nervous or something. It seems to take him a few seconds to recognise me, but when he does, his serious face breaks into a smile. He lifts the bottle in his hand towards me and gives a thumbs-up with his other hand. I give him a thumbs-up back and then he's quickly gone, lost within his dance.

Shelly and Diane's house is in a Victorian terrace, the kind of thing Mia would like. As Shelly opens the door and we all follow into the hallway, I notice a slight smell of damp. She and Eugene have been giggling all the way back in the taxi and they continue now, though at what I have no idea. Eugene has promised me that we're only coming here for one drink, then going back to Blackheath. I don't think I've ever looked forward to getting into my cold and lonely bed so much.

The living room is small and has a straw-like, almost wooden-looking rug on the floor. There is a tiny fireplace with decorated tiles. The house is nice, homely. Shelly drops onto the sofa, Eugene sits beside her and I stand awkwardly as Diane leaves the room and then comes back with cans of beer in her arms. She hands us one each. They're cold, but not cold enough to have been in a fridge. I open mine. I've had far too much to drink already and it tastes horrible. I take a few more gulps.

'Right, we're knackered. We're heading off to bed.' Eugene rests his hand on Shelly's back and looks at me.

I hate him right now. He knows I won't, can't protest in front of them. I can't remind him of his promise that their house was just a stop on our way home. I'd feel rude if I left on my own. Bastard.

They're gone from the room. Diane is looking at me.

'Let's go to bed,' she says, smiling. 'I'm knackered too.'

'Yeah, me too.' A fake yawn comes out of nowhere and ends far too soon and undramatically. 'That sofa looks comfy.'

'Don't be silly, you can't sleep on the sofa. Come upstairs with me.'

She takes my hand, which should feel odd but I'm too drunk to care. We go upstairs and I hope to God she's about to show me into a spare room. I trip on the top step and get my footing back just in time before I fall flat out. Beer spills from my can onto the carpet.

'I'm so sorry,' I whisper. I suddenly feel like I'm in a situation that I shouldn't be in, like I'm doing something wrong and if I speak too loudly I might get caught.

'Don't worry,' she whispers back.

Then she's gone through a door.

We lie in bed, both on our backs. I look at the ceiling and hope that she's fallen asleep. She hasn't spoken for a while now. I want her to fall asleep so much that I don't move or breathe too heavily so I don't prevent her from dozing off. I've undressed and I'm wearing only my boxer shorts. Her sheets feel inappropriate against my skin. They're clinging to me. I don't want to be here. I guess she's in her underwear too, though I'm not sure as I had my eyes closed as she got into bed, pretending an early attempt at sleep. The moment I got into her bed and felt her sheets against my skin, since we're laying side by side, I've had the most uncomfortable, unbearable arousal I've ever felt. I want it to go away but it's not even waning. It feels horrible, makes me cringe.

'Are you still awake?'

She turns her head towards me and I've been caught with my eyes open.

'Yes.'

For a moment there's silence between us again, the only sounds coming from Shelly's room.

'Don't you want to be with me?'

I lie still, feeling more out of control that I've ever felt with a woman other than Mia, and then I involuntarily turn to her, lean on my elbow and look down at her face. My hand reaches over and rests on her stomach. Her hair spills onto the pillows. It's the same length as Mia's, has its almost perfect straightness. In the near dark of the room it looks the same colour too, and I stroke her hair on the pillows, and just for a second, just for a second…

Eugene has the drawn expression I've seen so many times after he's had a night out, only now I've seen the cause of it first-hand. It's still early. In our half-drunk state we're surrounded by only the odd commuter. I guess they're all going in the other direction.

All night I could hear Eugene and Shelly, long after Diane and I had gone quiet. At one point there were cries and I had no idea if they were coming from her or from him. Going by what he tells me and Jessica on a regular basis, whether we want to hear it or not, he'll most likely be doing the same thing with a different woman by next week, if not sooner. Eugene is driven to find pleasure. In his tired face now it looks like a burden, like he's just fed an addiction. I'm sure that when he dies his soul will breathe a huge sigh of relief.

He turns and sees me looking at him. I look away quickly, but too late.

'So how was she?'

'How was who?' I know what he's talking about.

'Who the hell do you think I mean?'

'You mean Diane?'

'Yes!'

'Well she was nice enough. We chatted quite a bit in the end. We had to block out your noise somehow.'

'And?'

'And what?'

'What did she let you do?'

I'm wondering what to say next, considering how much truth I want to tell.

'Stop being so bloody secretive, Lewis, we can talk about this stuff.' He looks almost offended.

I glance to the seats opposite where a guy sits holding a paperback. I bet he's not reading a word of it now. I lower my voice in the hope that Eugene might do the same.

'Well, there's nothing much to tell, really.'

'Shut up!' he yells. 'Stop winding me up.' His smile begins to drop a little, then slowly he shakes his head from side to side, not taking his eyes off mine. 'No, Lewis, no, mate.'

'Nothing happened, OK?'

'What the hell do you mean nothing happened? She was

cooked and on the plate, mate!'

'Well, we're not all like you.'

'Yes *we* are.'

He looks confused. He's thinking about something.

'Was it, y'know,' he asks.

'Was it what?'

'Y'know.' He nods a couple of times towards my groin, which makes my knees come together a little.

I'm not answering him.

'Did you drink too much to get it up?'

'No!'

I've yelled. The guy opposite still hasn't turned a page.

'Well, what was it then?'

I realise now that he'd never understand it's because I couldn't. That I'm in love with someone, Mia, whom he's never even met. He'd never understand the connection of love taking over the thought of touching someone. There would have to be something physical for Eugene.

'OK, OK. I drank too much, OK?'

'Oh, mate,' he says, sighing. He shakes his head. 'It happens to the best of us, it happens to the best of us.'

As our train begins to move and cross the river, he looks out of the window as the beautiful view of London emerges, as if he's considering the effects of some awful affliction on mankind. Maybe he's just mourning the missed opportunity of pleasure on my behalf. He pulls up the hood on his jacket and rests his head on the shaking window.

THIRTY-NINE

I still feel tired from my night out with Eugene, even though two days have passed. The restaurant doesn't close for hours. I wish I could go home now and go to bed.

There are only a few customers here. A paint-splattered labourer tucking into a bacon sandwich. Two girls concentrating on their mobile phones. A middle-aged couple who don't speak or even look at each other while they eat. A woman walks through the door, goes to the far end of the restaurant and sits at the table near the sun-steered yucca. I wish she'd sat closer to me. I get up from my seat and, as I walk over to her, my legs ache.

'What can I get you?'

For a moment we both stare, then a feeling of great discomfort treads through me, like I've been caught doing something shameful again.

'Lewis?'

'Kelly.'

She's changed. I haven't seen her for so many years. I can see those years in her face. She looks good though. Beautiful even.

'God, I hardly recognised you. How are you?' She looks down over my body, all the way to my trainers, then slowly back up again. There's worry in her expression. She and Carl have the same eyes.

'I'm fine. What can I get you?' As the words tumble out, I feel rude, like I've cut her off.

'Oh.' She glances at the menu on the table but doesn't pick it up to read it properly. 'I'll have a sandwich and a coke, thanks.'

'What kind of sandwich?'

'Anything.'

She knows. I'll not have a chance on biding any time on sandwich fillings with her. I want to get away. 'OK, I'll come back in a minute.' I try to reclaim some of my rudeness.

'Great,' she says. A little smile appears at the sides of her lips.

I walk quickly towards the kitchen doors and I'm so shaken from seeing her I feel as though I might fall. I can barely put one foot in front of the other.

I pass the order to Jessica.

'There's nothing written on it, Lewis.'

'Just give me a sandwich and a coke.'

'What kind of sandwich?'

'Anything.'

'What the hell's up with you?'

'Sorry, I've just seen someone I didn't expect to, that's all.'

She peers through the square service hole into the restaurant.

'A woman!' She's surprised. Delighted, too.

'Oh no, it's nothing like that.'

'Where's there a woman?' Eugene looks up from his newspaper. He's sitting on the food preparation worktop, has been since he arrived.

'It's nothing, honestly, an old family friend, that's all.' Then I think. How did Kelly know I was here? None of them know where I am. 'Do you mind if I take a quick break?'

'Of course not.' Jessica is distracted now, sorting through the fridge.

Eugene has gone back to reading his newspaper.

I walk to Kelly's table. She's looking out of the window, then up at me as I sit opposite her.

'OK, honest answer this time please. How are you?'

'I'm not too bad. So you know then.'

'Of course I do.'

I sigh and my hand reaches for my forehead, rubs it a few times.

'I'm so sorry, Lewis. You must be going through hell.'

'Something like that. How did you know I'd be here?'

'I didn't. I'm just in the area for a meeting with my publisher.'

I notice now that she's in smart dress. She looks great, like a businesswoman and as strong as ever.

'How are your novels going?'

'Good thanks. I'm about to get my fourth published, hence the meeting.'

'Congratulations. I loved the last one.'

'You read it?'

'Yes, of course. I've read all of them.'

She seems surprised. I don't know why.

'Are you managing to sort anything out with Mia yet?'

The sound of her name makes me feel guilty as my mind jumps back to my night out with Eugene. Diane. The lying in bed. The inappropriateness of sheets.

'No. I've not seen her properly since. I've only seen Carl once.'

'Yes, I saw him later that night. I had to go and pick him up from A&E.'

Guilt again, as I close my eyes and see his blood dripping onto the pavement in the beer garden. Four punches. His hands covering his face. Him not fighting back. I wish he had now.

'Is he OK?'

'He's fine.' She doesn't seem annoyed at what has happened, at what I've done. 'He was a shit, he knows that.'

'That's one word for him. I can think of others.'

'I'm sure you can.'

Eugene brings her sandwich and coke and unashamedly checks her out. As he puts the plate and glass on the table and she looks down at it, he takes a really good look down her top.

'Thank you, lovely,' she says.

'Lovely, you're welcome.' He turns and winks at me as he walks away, and I notice Jessica's head sticks out from the kitchen doors, like someone peering between the curtains of a stage.

'I'll leave you in peace while you eat your lunch.' I move to stand from the table, but as I do so, she puts her hand on mine.

'No, stay for a little while. If it won't get you into any trouble. Have half my sandwich.'

'I've eaten, thanks,' I lie.

She takes a bite. 'So where are you living then, Lewis?'

'I don't want anyone to know where I'm living.'

'It's not anyone, it's me. I won't even tell them I've seen you if you don't want me to.'

'I don't.'

'No problem.'

'I'm living just up the road, renting some rooms in a house.'

'Is it OK?'

I nod.

'Have you got everything you need?'

'Yeah.'

'Do you need money? I mean a loan, until you get back on your feet.'

I feel like her little brother's friend again. There's a

maternal quality to her questions. For some reason, I remember the toad we caught and put in her bedroom.

'No I'm fine, thank you. My pay from here is enough to keep me going. How are your parents? I often think of them.'

As she speaks, I'm at ease. I watch, listen, appreciate the comfort of seeing a familiar face and hearing a familiar voice. When she was young, she was always trying to look different, wearing too much make-up and having weird hairstyles. Now she's a woman, her look is basic, exquisitely plain. Her hair is dark blonde and straight. Earrings move as she speaks, little squiggles with a ball on the end, like silver tadpoles dangling by their tales. She's formidable, like she always was, and though she's being gentle towards me now, there's still bitch-potential in her eyes.

'Sorry, am I boring you?' She waits for an answer.

'What?'

'You zoned out on me for a minute there.'

'Sorry, I'm just a bit tired from a night out.'

'Well I'm pleased to hear you're going out.'

She finishes her lunch and puts a ten pound note on the table.

'Here's my card,' she says, producing one from her bag. 'If you need anything, get in touch, OK?'

'Thank you.'

'Once you've had enough time, do try to talk to Mia. Things can't be left as they are forever.'

'Do you know all about it?'

'Yes, but only after you met with him. He called me to pick him up from the hospital, and then it all came out. He called Mum and Dad too.'

'And Mia?'

'They've not seen or spoken to each other since the morning you saw them together, I believe.'

I find an unexpected sadness at hearing this. It really is all over between the three of us.

Kelly stands and pulls on her coat. 'Even though what he's done is awful, you know there's no bad in him, don't you?'

I think of Carl, of his eyes with so much going on behind them. His expression when he thought no one was looking at him. The expression which told that something was crashing down inside him. Maybe if I'd pushed harder, tried harder, he might have been able to tell me before any of this happened.

Kelly still looks at me.

'Will you ever be able to speak to him again?'

'I don't know.'

She leans down and embraces me unexpectedly, putting her arms quickly around my neck and resting her hands firmly on my back. I feel uncomfortable and put my hands politely on her shoulders, until, slowly, my face falls into her hair and my heart into the comfort of home and a beautiful moment of peace transpires even more unexpected than the hug.

She lets go and kisses me quickly on the cheek. 'Keep in touch, Lewis.'

She walks away, and then she's gone.

'Oh yes!' Eugene yells, making me and all of the customers turn to look at him. Like his team just scored a goal, he's jumping a little and holding a thumbs-up in the air towards me with both hands. I smile at him in despair as he looks alternately between me and Jessica, nodding enthusiastically at whatever idea is going through his mind.

FORTY

My weight is plummeting. There are greyish patches under my eyes and I hope that Jessica doesn't notice them. It's the first time anyone has ever asked if they can draw me and I look my worst. I've regretted saying yes since she asked me. I dread to see how she sees me. The only reason I'm looking forward to it being finished is so that I don't have to sit here any longer. Eugene lies on her bed, hands behind his head, looking at the ceiling.

'I've got your eyes now, I think.' She doesn't look up.

'Oh, OK.' I suddenly feel awkward about my eyes, and though I keep my head still, I quickly look around the room. I don't want to move, even though she's told me I can.

'They're the most difficult I've ever drawn.'

'That's because they're so messed up from all that drink.' Eugene looks to me, then back at the ceiling. I don't think he's joking or being nasty, he's probably just being honest. Honesty is something that comes out of him without much thought, or consideration.

'Lewis has got lovely eyes. They're much brighter than yours.'

Eugene lifts his head and squints at me in concentration for a moment.

'They're difficult for me to draw because they have a really great depth. They look completely different from one minute to the next.'

I don't even know if that's true, but I tense at how much she's been studying me. At how she could think something so personal.

The only sounds now are Eugene's breathing – which is always audible in a quiet room – the scrape of Jessica's pencil and the waves of rain that the wintery wind is throwing against the window. The mist that stuck around for days has cleared now.

It's in these quiet moments that I become most aware of what is going on in my life, of who I am with, who I am not with. It's not good for me to have these thoughts. If I was at home now I'd get myself a drink, but I'm not and I don't feel I can ask Jessica or Eugene for one either. It's only midday, on a Sunday. I remember the cup of tea that Eugene made for me when I arrived. I look down at it on the floor beside my chair. It has a milky film on its surface now. It's been there ages.

'Are you getting used to your place a bit more now?' Jessica glances between the paper and my face.

'Yes,' I lie. 'I'm gradually getting used to it. I like Blackheath a lot. It feels so familiar already, like I've lived here for years. The house is just taking a bit of getting used to.'

'It's bloody spooky that house, and that's just the outside.' Eugene looks at Jessica. 'Maybe he'll actually invite us around one day, eh?'

'I will when I've got it more sorted out, definitely.'

'We went shopping for all that stuff though. Is it not looking more homely now?' I think he's trying to be nice. He looks back to the ceiling. 'You know there's loads of bodies out there, don't you?'

'What?'

'Buried under the heath, in front of your house. There's thousands of bodies buried there, from the plague.'

'That's just a myth.' Jessica has slowed, only a gentle scrape of her pencil every few seconds now.

'It's not. It's true. They're under the grass right in front of your house, where your front windows look out.'

Jessica stops drawing and looks at Eugene.

I think of how many times I've walked across the heath, where the crows stand and sulk. Where people are trying to rest.

'Stop trying to freak him out!'

Eugene pulls an expression as if he's been accused of something he knows nothing about. Then his face relaxes again. 'You're right, though. Blackheath is lovely. I like it most now, in the winter. I feel like I've lived here for years too.'

'You have. Right, I think I've finished.' Jessica smiles at the page.

Eugene jumps from the bed and goes to her. We'd both been banned from looking while she was drawing.

'Oh wow, that's brilliant. You're really good.' Eugene puts his arm around her in an unusual, non-sarcastic way. 'You're going to be impressed with this, mate.' He looks at me with certainty.

I wait in dread as Jessica puts her hands around the board she's been leaning on, ready to turn it towards me. I close my eyes, a very long blink. When the picture turns, I gasp. Then a little unexpected laugh comes out. I lean forward, try to concentrate on what I'm seeing. 'Oh my God.'

They look at each other, awkwardly confused, then back at me.

'Don't you like it?' she asks.

'Yes, it's brilliant, it's just…'

'Just what?'

'Well, it's amazing. It looks so much like someone I know.' As I look more, I see him more. Our eyes are the same, even the slight vertical line between the eyebrows, which I'd hardly noticed on myself before, but which I now know is there. Though with my older age and now longer and scruffier hair, from every part of the face, the more I look, the more he looks back at me.

'Yeah, it reminds you of yourself, you dickhead!' Eugene says.

'No, it reminds me of a friend of mine, really.'

'But you like it though?' Jessica is smiling expectantly.

'Yes, I do. I really love it. Thank you.' I'm pleased if I look like him.

Jessica holds the picture and Eugene stands behind her with his hand on her shoulder. They smile and giggle as if showing someone the first picture of their first child.

Still bewildered, I look back at the drawing, captivated by the young man looking back at me.

FORTY-ONE

On the bench beside the pond, it's cold and I'm wrapped up against the weather. Over the past few days, the last of the leaves have fallen, like the trees had realised that autumn had ended and suddenly dropped everything in their hands. The leaves run across the heath now, making the invisible wind apparent. There's not a flower in sight. All the scents of summer and autumn have been extinguished.

I open my book. It's a novel I bought in a charity shop in the village earlier today, about a man in Victorian times who moved to the countryside to establish a school. I didn't realise until after I'd chosen it that when I lived in Whiteflower Woods I'd read stories about people who lived in exciting cities, and since I've moved to London, I've chosen to read the opposite.

I've tried to read the first page several times but haven't got any further than the first paragraph. I've taken nothing of it in. Understood nothing. Now I can't get beyond the first couple of sentences before my mind wanders back to Mia and Carl and I realise now that I don't want to read again. I don't want to imagine things or learn. Nothing new is being formed within me now. I just keep on going over the events of the past, trying to make sense of them. I'm remembering things but taking nothing from them, like from the first page of the book. I close its cover for the last time, look over the stillness of the pond and try to think of something else.

Today's shift got busy and I'm tired. I think I need to drink some tea or something before I have any whisky tonight. I don't feel well again. I have pain in my head every day now. My legs ache and my arms ache even more. My energy has gone and been replaced by a dull, heavy burden. I can feel the veins and muscles in my arms. It's not that they're aching too, but I just feel aware of them, strangely aware that they're under my skin, doing things, working, or struggling to work. It's as if my body, like Blackheath now, is going into its own winter.

Seeing Kelly last week has made me think of Mum and Dad. They must have called the house in Putney since I left and I've not answered their calls to my mobile. I wonder what Mia has told them. I feel guilty at ignoring their calls and having not returned them, and I feel now that I should. Not that I want to, but that I should. I have no signal on my mobile again, though I usually get one here on the heath. I walk back to the restaurant and change a ten pound note into coins from the till.

The payphone is on the edge of the heath in a red box, not far from the pond. I pick up the receiver. It's clunky. I've not used one of these for years and I remember the nights that I used to spend hours on the one in Whiteflower, calling Mia. I wonder if Carl loved her then, as he sat outside on the kerb, waiting for me.

I put several pound coins in and they drop loudly. I dial the number and hear a distant ringing tone, imagine their phone ringing through the house in the woods.

'Lewis!' Mum sounds happy to hear from me. 'I know something has happened. I've called the house several times and Mia always says you're out and I know you're never out without her and why haven't you been picking up your mobile?'

'I'm not at home at the moment, Mum. I've moved out.'

'What do you mean you've moved out?'

'Mia and I have separated, I think. I'd rather wait and tell you and Dad about it when I see you.'

'Oh right, I see.'

I can tell in her voice that she doesn't want to be so far away. I hear Dad in the background, asking if I'm OK, and she mutters something which I can't hear properly. There's a moment of silence and I know what's coming next.

'I'll come and see you, OK?'

'No, Mum, no need. I'll come and visit you.'

'Where are you living?'

'I'm in a different part of London now. I'm in Blackheath.'

'Blackheath?'

'Yes, it's a lovely place.'

'Oh. Why Blackheath?' Her voice has changed. Instead of gentle, inquisitive.

'Well it just sort of happened really. I'm living in a great house. It's really new and smart. It's right on the edge of the heath, Yarrow Road. It's really one of the nicest spots I've ever seen in the whole of London and everything is going really well.' I almost believe myself.

'Yarrow Road,' Mum says, not as a question, but confirming it out loud for herself.

'Yes.'

'Which number?'

'Which number what?'

'Which number house?'

I realise now I'm giving her my exact address, which I'd never intended to do, though I know she'll want to send things through the post.

'Number 28.'

Mum lets out a little laugh, almost hysterical, and it ends in a sort of choke. I hear Dad speaking again in the background, but I still can't hear him.

'Is this some kind of sick joke?' Her words have slowed, like she's drunk.

'What?'

I hear movement, noise down the line, like the phone has been dropped and picked up again.

'Why are you doing this, Lewis?'

'Doing what?' I panic, feel more awake than I've felt all day, but my legs tremble. I feel vulnerable now, on the edge of the vast heath, in a glass box.

'How did you know?' She's angry now.

'Know what, Mum?'

'You know what I'm talking about. Why? Is this some kind of sick, fucking joke?'

I've never heard her swear. She hasn't yelled at me since I was a child. She yells and screams and I put the phone down. In the silence of the box I realise I'm desperately out of breath, like I've just been chased.

FORTY-TWO

'So how are you and your friend Jessica getting along then?'

Parker is sitting in his usual position on the living room floor, leaning back with his arms stretched out and his palms flat on the floorboards. I don't know how he doesn't find them too cold. Stamp is curled up and snoring lightly beside him.

'Yeah, we get along well.'

'Do you like her? As more than a friend, I mean.'

Whenever he asks me these personal questions, I always feel a moment's hesitation. I wonder why he's interested. I feel guarded at telling too much to someone who I know so little about, to someone so young. Sometimes, I wish he was older. I never had a problem talking to Carl about these things.

'I don't think so.'

'Well, if you get along well, maybe you should give it a try to get to know her a little better.'

'What?'

'I don't just mean like that. Well, that as well, I suppose, but not just that.'

'Well…' I can't think of what to say next.

'Ah, so you have thought about it!'

I feel a smile grab at my face. 'But I think those thoughts about most women. It doesn't mean I want to do anything about it. It's out of bounds really.'

'Why?'

'Because she's my friend. And, more importantly, I'm married.'

'You're separated.'

'But still married.'

I think about how that didn't stop Mia and Carl. Maybe Parker thinks the same thing as he looks at me thoughtfully, with a very slight look of annoyance, which I think he's trying to hide.

Parker's gaze falls to the fireplace, where the fire has died down. Only an occasional flicker of a flame dances out above the remains of the logs. This is the first time it's been lit since I moved in, but it's so cold tonight that we decided to prise the boards off it and hope the chimney was clean. I really should have asked Mrs Moore first, but luckily it hasn't smoked the house out. There is warmth in front of the fire, but the rest of the room is still cold. The scent of flowers in here is stronger than ever. I still haven't found where it's coming from.

I watch Parker as he picks a couple of logs from the pile. He places them in the fire confidently. I can tell that he has grown up in a house with a fireplace, like I did. He turns and looks at me. I see the slight vertical line between his eyebrows and remember Jessica's drawing. I can see myself in his features now, though I can't pinpoint exactly where all the similarities lie. In the green of his eyes, the shape of his cheeks. We don't look identical though. He looks healthy. His skin glows and his features are strong. He's handsome. I realise we're looking at each other and haven't said a word. He doesn't smile like he usually does. He's seeing something in my face too, like something from deep within him looks deeply into me. I find it difficult to look away from him.

To break the moment, I go to the kitchen and get two more bottles of beer from the fridge. We've drunk a lot already. When I walk back into the living room I speak without having thought about what I'm going to say. It feels so good to talk.

'I just wouldn't know about getting to know another woman in that kind of way. Friends are fine. I'm not scared of women or anything, but more than that, well, I can see myself never having another relationship now.'

Parker looks at me in disbelief.

'And what age are you now?'

'I'm thirty-three.'

'Bit early to call it a day with all that, don't you think?'

'Well, it's how I feel.'

It really is how I feel now, but I feel childish at standing my ground about it.

Parker, unbothered about me speaking sternly, gets more comfortable on the floor and is almost in a sleeping position, his hands prayer-like and protecting his head from the floorboards. Stamp sighs heavily at whatever he's dreaming of. He's hardly moved all evening.

I lie on the sofa and look at the ceiling.

'I'm not saying you're wrong to feel that way,' Parker says. 'Really, I'm not, but do you ever wonder why it can make people feel that way? Being cheated on, I mean.'

'Feel what way?'

'That it can be so upsetting. When they're with someone, people generally can't cope with them having anything physical with someone else – it has to be one on one for most people. It would have to be that way for me too, to be honest. But I'm just saying, why do we feel like that?'

'It's just what happens when you love someone, I guess.' I don't have any other explanation to offer him.

'We get possessive?'

'I don't think it's possessiveness.'

He thinks for a moment. 'Well it is really. I mean, why shouldn't people be able to, or why should people have a problem with, someone they love having physical pleasure with someone else?'

I hate hearing the words *physical pleasure*, and I feel my body tense. I think of how much of an opinion Parker has on the subject for someone so young.

'How old are you?'

He hesitates, like he's having to think about it.

'I'm nineteen.'

I knew he was young, but hearing it makes our age difference more real. He must think I'm old. When I was a teenager, I thought thirty-three was old. He must think I'm silly. A weak man. I think about whether I am old enough to be his father. It doesn't feel that long ago that I was nineteen and thought I knew about love. I had just met Mia then. I realise now that those years since were my life. The time of knowing about love to not believing in it. Parker has such thoughtful views on it. I know something must have happened to him to have made him this way.

'Have you ever been in love?' I can ask this. He's asked me so much.

'I'm in love with someone now.'

I don't know what to say.

'But, it's not about whether someone is still in a relationship now. People don't fall out of love just because they leave someone, or someone leaves them. It's about having had the experience of it. If you'd stayed married, who knows, in twenty years' time you might not have wanted to have spent all of those years of your life with her.'

'I don't think that would have happened.'

'But what I'm saying is, you had it. You loved, and you were loved back. You don't seem to realise that, but when you do, you'll find some peace in what has happened. It's over, but today still happened. Today is still your life. Don't waste it on being bitter.'

His gaze falls to the fire again. He enjoys watching the flames, like I do. For a moment, or maybe it's minutes, there's only the sound of the rumbling and cracking of logs as they begin to burn.

I feel drunk now. I lie back on the sofa and rest my head on the arm and watch the flames grow. 'Parker, I don't feel well.'

The pain in my head has come on suddenly. Parker moves towards me and kneels beside the sofa. My eyes close. His hand is running through my hair and it feels good. It's easing the pain. It reminds me of being a child, and how, when I was unwell, Mum would stroke my head to make me feel better. Parker's hand through my hair is making me sleepy.

I wake gently, looking at the ceiling, remembering Parker telling me that I had loved. The pain has eased and I feel clear again now. Maybe he's right. Maybe I will be able to find some peace from this. Every time I speak to Parker, I feel better. Things make more sense when I speak to him. I think that's why he's here, why he's in my living room right now. He's come to help me. I want to tell him how, in our few meetings, he has helped. Even though I can't feel it yet, he's telling me to appreciate things, and I think that in time I might be able to. I find comfort in his words. Peace even, like he said.

I turn. As I lie and watch the flames, I realise that our conversation tonight has brought me more peace than any other we've had. I'm just beginning to see, just a glimmer of it, that perhaps I am fortunate, rather than ill-fated, because of Mia and Carl and everything that's happened between us. Maybe I could feel at peace with everything I'm leaving behind.

Suddenly, I remember. I've not told Parker about seeing him in the nightclub when I was out with Eugene. I lift my head and look down to him lying on the floor, but his eyes are closed.

'Parker,' I whisper, but he's asleep, his face serenely at rest. I stand up from the sofa and put the throw over him, gently tuck it around his shoulders. It'll get even colder during the small hours.

I go to the bedroom, pick up the blanket off the bed and take it into the living room. I want to sleep in here with them tonight. It's the right thing to do. His company feels so natural I could sleep in the same room as him every night. I lie on the sofa and pull the blanket over me, nearly covering my face. Near my feet, I feel Stamp jump up on the sofa and position himself for sleeping again. As he settles I feel his warmth and the gentle thump-thump of his little heart through the blanket. Calmly, I begin to fall asleep.

Daylight fills the room. My head hurts, but it's not a revengeful, pounding hangover. I turn and look down. Parker's not here, the throw lies strewn on the floor where he slept. I smile at his elusive exits. I don't need to look around to see if he's anywhere in the house. I can't feel his presence at all. He's gone.

In the kitchen, I fill the kettle, and as it boils I think of last night. It felt so good at the end. He gave me such a feeling of comfort. I try to remember his words, so I can feel them again. The kettle clicks, sending clouds of steam into the chilly morning air.

I wrap both my hands around the thick warm mug and sip. As I remember our conversation, I realise this might be the first time I've had such a sense of waking up since I found Mia and Carl tangled together. I'm waking quickly. My eyes are wide open.

Back in the living room, I sit on the sofa. As I look up, I freeze in shock.

I slowly put my mug down on the floor, but I don't take my eyes off the fireplace. The wooden boards are nailed across it.

'Why's he done that?' I whisper.

I kneel in front of the fireplace, run my finger over the smooth flat heads of the nails which hold the planks of wood tightly against the mantel. I'm so confused. Why has Parker nailed the boards back across? How didn't he wake me as I slept a few steps away on the sofa?

In the kitchen, I take the hammer from the drawer. The hammer that Parker had taken out of the drawer last night. I prise the boards from the mantel. It's the same cracking sound I heard last night when Parker prised them off. When the boards are on the floor, I feel sick as I rub my hand over the cold, clean hearth. There's been no fire lit here for years. There isn't even a grate here now.

But I watched Parker light it.

I felt its warmth on my face.

I watched the gentle light from its flames dance around the walls.

There is a huddle of empty beer bottles beside the sofa, but none on the floor where Parker had laid. I go to the kitchen to see where he's left them, but they're nowhere. I open the fridge and see more beer bottles than I expected, full and unopened. But how many were there? I don't know if there's too many bottles or not.

I walk back into the living room, sit on the sofa and hold my face in my hands.

'You're OK,' I tell myself. 'You're OK, you're OK, you're OK.'

FORTY-THREE

I need to speak to Mrs Moore. I think she's the only one who can give me answers. The only one who can help me understand what is happening to me and this house. Am I imagining things? I can't be.

The night Jessica saw someone in my living room on the webcam. Then, afterwards, when I heard someone in the loft, Mrs Moore knew something. I'm sure of it. I know there was no one in the house. I know there was no one in the loft. But she knew. She told me not to be afraid, or not to run. I can't remember. Her words made sense, I remember that.

I need to speak to her.

I've had to leave the living room as I can't bear to look at the clean fireplace. I don't want to walk downstairs yet, so I stand on the landing, at the window. The bare heath is speaking to me, telling me that nothing about last night really happened. If that's true, then neither did the feeling of comfort I felt from speaking to Parker. It's gone now, and that was the only thing I've found to hold onto.

I'm not sure now if I want to speak to Mrs Moore, to ask

her things or hear her answers. I don't want her to touch my face the way she does when she speaks to me. She always looks at me worriedly when she does that and it makes me feel worse, though I must speak to her. I must ask her what's going on. I know she knows.

On the first staircase, the pain in my head suddenly appears and my head pounds. This can't just be a hangover. I feel so sick. Life is draining from me. I stop and put my hand on the bannister on the first-floor landing. My sight is hazy. For a few seconds it's gone completely. I take a few deep breaths, and it clears again, like mist in a light breeze.

I stand outside the door to the basement flat. The fire in the hallway has died down, just a bumpy mound of black and grey with an orange glow. I take a log from the basket and place it on top of the embers. She'll only ask me to when she opens the door anyway.

I straighten myself and then knock twice. Just the ticking of the clock that I can never find. Then I hear some movement from the other side of the door. Slowly, it opens.

'I was wondering when you'd come asking questions,' she says.

She looks a little lost, as if she's not sure if she's pleased to see me or not, but then she smiles. I don't know what to say. We just look at each other.

'In fact, I've been wanting to speak with you,' she says. 'Come in.'

In her living room there are two armchairs, one on each side of the fireplace. She sits in what must be her usual chair, as it has worn, flattened cushions on it. She lowers herself slowly onto them. I sit in the other chair. The fire is roaring. On top of the mantel is a clock with a small bunch of browned, dried flowers either side of it. The carpet is darkly patterned. Directly outside the window is a brick wall, but near the top, the sky. I wonder again why she lives in the basement, in such a dull part of this big house.

Mrs Moore makes a pot of tea. It's the first time I've

seen anyone make a pot of tea since I was a child. Like Aunt Ruth used to have, she has a table beside her armchair with a kettle and all the necessary. She makes the tea ceremoniously, pours while neither of us speak.

I notice the clock on her mantel is silent. Its hands are still. There's nothing except for the rumble of flames and the clinking of her stirring spoon against china.

'When I saw you in the hallway that night, and you told me I was afraid, what did you mean?'

She looks up, though not as far as the ceiling. 'I know you're not settled. There's something wrong, isn't there?' She looks down at her dress, flattens out non-existent creases, as if she's approaching a delicate subject and can't look me in the eye as she does so.

'Something wrong with me?'

'You been living here like a ghost for the past weeks.'

'I try to pass by your door quietly, so I don't disturb you.'

'I know.' She seems grateful at the thought. 'You're meant to be here. Everything is at peace in this house. You know that, don't you?'

'I'm sorry, I don't think I understand what you mean.' My head is aching.

'Patrick brought you here.'

'No, he didn't.' I shudder from hearing the name again. 'I found my own way here. I don't even know anyone called Patrick.'

'You found your way here on your own?' She smiles, as if I've said something silly.

'Because I answered your advert for the rooms.'

'I never placed an advert.' She looks surprised. 'Why would I? I don't need money. I've no one to spend money on.'

'Of course you placed the advert. I wrote down your address after speaking to you on the phone in that hotel I was staying in.'

'I don't have a phone, Lewis. I've never had a phone in my life. They're too … noisy.'

I rub my face and it slightly eases the pain in my head. I can't remember if I spoke to Mrs Moore on the phone at all. I try to picture it. I was standing in the hotel foyer at a payphone. Everything felt different then. I realised I couldn't go home and was calling around trying to find somewhere to live. I spoke to a woman with a flat in Hackney, a man needing a lodger in Lewisham. Why did I leave that hotel and get on a boat to Greenwich? Was I alone?

'So why did you let me move in here?' I feel like an intruder now, sitting somewhere I've not been invited.

'It was the first time anyone had rung that doorbell for years. I was amazed it still worked.'

'Mrs Moore, please. Why did you let me in?'

She thinks for a moment. I don't think she's finding this conversation easy.

'Because, as soon as I saw you, I knew who you were.' She sighs with relief, like she's just got something off her chest.

My hands shake. I put them on the arms of the chair to steady myself.

Still she looks at me, says nothing.

'I have to go now.' I need to move out of this house.

'Very well,' she says. Her voice tells me she's disappointed that I'm not asking more questions. 'You know where I am if you need me.'

But I can't stay.

I think this might be the last time I'll see her. I don't even know her. She sits upright, properly, like a woman of her age might say you should. A lady having someone round for tea, like there's nothing wrong here at all. Like I'm not sitting here in front of her, shaking. Why do I find her so hard to read? Like our age difference makes her remote. I never felt this with Aunt Ruth.

On the shelf beside me, I notice a photo. There are

framed photos all over the house. I've walked past them countless times and never stopped to look. They blend in so much that it's like they're part of the walls, part of the system and structure which holds the house together. The picture beside me is old, its colour faded in its wooden frame. Speckled with dust.

'It can't be him,' I think, but I've whispered it. I speak to the picture, to the man who's almost still a boy. He holds Stamp under his arm and smiles broadly at the camera with the cheeky, mischievous grin I've seen so many times. Mrs Moore, much, much younger, smiling. She wraps her arm around his shoulder lovingly.

'Mrs Moore, who is this with you in the photo?'

'You know who it is. It's my son.' Her eyes glisten. 'Did your mother never show you a photo of him, in all these years?'

'I don't know what you mean.'

'He'd have made you smile. I wish you could have met him.' She looks at me, waiting for an answer. Waiting for me to correct her. 'He died in 1979. Three weeks before you were born.'

Somehow, I already know what she is saying. How do I know?

'Patrick?' I ask.

'Yes.'

'Parker?'

She nods, my grandmother.

She's close to tears.

My face has gone numb. I've been speaking with the dead.

There's a cracking sound, small but definite. It came from her. My gaze falls on her brooch, the one she always wears. A dragonfly inside an oval of pale yellow glass. Such an old-styled thing to wear. I imagine Aunt Ruth wearing it, not to be fashionable, but unfashionable, buying it from a box of junk at a car boot sale, and I giggle. It cracks again and I gasp. She looks down, then slowly back at me, confused. A line runs vertically down the brooch now.

'Lewis, whatever's the matter?'

'Mrs Moore!' I point to her brooch.

She looks down and then back at me once again. She doesn't see what I see.

The dragonfly is moving. Its spindly legs are stretching backwards and forwards. Its wings twitch. Slowly, it crawls between the crack, like it's hatching. It sits on top of its broken yellow glass egg, looks around with its dark, helmet-like eyes. It's trying to fly.

I brush my hand over Mrs Moore's chest and knock the dragonfly to the floor. It just sits there, transparent wings beating madly, metallic blue tail rising and gently falling.

'Lewis!'

She has her arms raised now, her knuckles protruding. They shield her face as she leans against the back of her armchair, like she thinks I'm about to hit her.

'Stop it!' she yells, but her voice makes hardly any sound at all. 'Lewis, you need to see a doctor. I'm worried about you.'

I walk backwards towards the door, stunned. I've frightened her, and I have no idea why she's talking about there being something wrong with me, and now I'm frightened too. I don't know what I've done.

On the floor, the dragonfly is still trying to remember how to fly.

I rush from the house and down the steps, cross the road quickly without looking. I begin to run across the heath and only realise after I've passed him that the man is sitting on the bench again. Just for a second I look over my shoulder as I run. He sits in his usual spot on the bench, wearing his mac and hat, looking out into nothing.

There's only the thud of my trainers on the frosty grass breaking the silence of the heath. My breath pants white and I begin to feel calmer. I see the traffic from the main road some distance to my right, but I can't hear it. 'You're OK,' I tell myself, running in a straight line across the heath. 'You're OK, you're OK, you're OK.' I feel more and more at ease as I get further away from the house, from the dragonfly, from the photo and away from what I've just discovered. I frightened her. I run in longer strides now. I'm flying across the heath like the sulking crows I've disturbed and who are now also looking for a new place to rest.

At the other side of the heath, I stop where the pathway alongside the road begins. I turn, look back at the house. It sits distantly, the slight mist which has just fallen making it look even further away than it really is. I can hardly see it now. A safe distance.

I walk along the path, further away from the house and all the things it's home to.

FORTY-FOUR

I walk the streets of Greenwich. Most people must be at work as the pathways are quiet. I've texted Michael and told him I won't be at work today as I'm sick. I am sick.

I'm away from Blackheath now, away from that house. There's something so wrong with that house. A lonely feeling. Leaving it has made no difference though. The feeling has followed me.

In the market, I remember being here with Mia and Carl. I know I'll never be here with them again. I know, and it's broken me, that they are both out of my life now. I try to remember the feeling that I felt last night in my conversation with Parker, but I don't want to think about Parker. I can't think of him as my father. Is he in that house now, or walking Stamp over the heath? He isn't there. He couldn't have been there last night. I must have dreamed it. This is the version of myself I must live with now. This is what losing Mia and Carl has done to me.

But did Mrs Moore know I was her grandson all along?

I can't think about it.

I sit in a pub. It's quiet and there are only a few people

here. I order pints of lager and whisky at the same time, down the whisky then drink the pint. As soon as it's half gone I order more. It feels good.

I walk again. It's colder now. The streets, busier. The sky has clouded and I don't think I will see the sun anymore today. Dusk is gathering over Greenwich. Christmas lights have been lit. They hang across the roads from one building to another. Big, silver stars dangle from lampposts. I don't want to think about Christmas. It seems impossible.

I text Eugene and ask if he can meet me for breakfast tomorrow. I need to tell him what has happened. I need to tell him that I had a conversation with someone last night, but there was no one there and I don't know what's wrong. I remember the time Parker sat next to me on the bench beside the pond, the time we ran across the heath to escape the rainstorm, the time he stayed over and I heard him crying in the night.

'Did I imagine it all?'

I realise I've spoken and stop in the middle of the pavement. Crowds of people are passing by me. I feel like I don't exist at all.

The river. There are tourists here, people walking with their children, couples walking hand in hand. People are sitting outside pubs, wrapped in coats and scarves and gloves against the winter, which is getting colder by the minute. I walk as far along the river as I can, until I know I have to turn back.

I buy a can of lager in a shop and open it as soon as I'm out of the door. I take a mouthful and then I remember. The feeling of peace I had last night. Parker helped me see the glimmer of a feeling that I'm getting over this. I look down at the can in my hand. I never used to drink much before I realised what was happening between Mia and Carl. He was right. I did know what was going on between them. I've known for years. I walk to a rubbish bin and drop the can into it. Then I take a few deep breaths. I need to sober up. I need to think. If I don't go back to Blackheath for the night, then I'm homeless.

I don't want to walk anymore and I wait at a bus stop. Crowds of people gather and push to board when buses arrive. Rush hour is well underway. I rest against a wall.

I remember now. Last night when I felt unwell and I laid on the sofa. Parker touched my hair. It eased the pain in my head. And beside the pond, the first time we met. He shook my hand when he introduced himself and I'd felt intimidated by him. I felt his warmth. I look down at my hand, turn it over to see my palm and the underside of my fingers. He touched them. I felt him. He was there. Why didn't he tell me who he was?

'Do the dead keep secrets?'

At the bus stop, a woman turns and then looks away quickly. Beside her, a little girl stares at me. The woman puts her hand around the girl's shoulder and turns her away.

A crow approaches me, taking jumping steps across the pavement towards my trainers. When it stops it looks up, as if waiting for me to say something. We look at each other, in recognition. The crows. I remember the night I returned from Jessica and Eugene's place and found the house covered with crows. Mrs Moore said they were there because of me.

My legs ache as I walk now. The buses are too crowded. It will take a while to get to Blackheath from here, but I don't want to get back too soon. I see an occasional white flake drifting in a new breeze, which is getting stronger. The snow is coming. I wrap my coat around me, crossing over each side of the zip and folding my arms over them to keep it shut. Trees are shaking in the wind now, their naked winter branches rustling against each other. A cyclist passes me, wrapped in rain gear and struggling to stay on his bike.

I wonder whether Parker will be in the house when I get there and, if he is, whether he will ever appear to me again. I don't believe in ghosts. But I shook his hand. I must believe in what I touch. And the glimpse he gave me, that I can leave Mia and Carl behind and have peace. I saw it. He showed it to me.

I look across the heath. It's dark. A stream of traffic flows down the road but the heath is a sheet of black, with lights from houses around the sides. I see, far away, the row of houses in which my home is. I count them, the tiny buildings, from the end of the road in which they stand, to find mine.

I must be mistaken. I count again.

Far away, the lights in my rooms are switched on. My heart races and I begin to walk at speed. Mrs Moore. I frightened her this morning. Maybe she has asked for help to get me out of the house. Maybe when I arrive she'll have neighbours there to tell me not to come back. She might have called the police. I'd forgotten that I'd frightened her, to the point where she held her hands up to shield her face.

I break into a run, not bothering with the pathways but going straight across the dark grass, the same way I ran away from the house this morning.

I fall suddenly and heavily and hit my chin. I wipe my face and arms and feel wetness. I feel no pain. I spit over and over again. I find comfort in this taste of blood in my mouth. On my knees, I look towards the house. It's getting closer now.

I stand at the bottom of the steps. I can see no one through the windows, so I open the door. The fire in the hallway is warming as I run up the stairs. In my rooms, all the lights are on. Living room, bathroom, kitchen, bedroom, empty room.

I stand on the landing.

'Parker.'

But there's no one here. There's just the silence, between the tick-tocks of the clock that I can never find. Time doesn't exist in this house. It's just make-believe.

In the bedroom I switch the light off, close the door and

sit on my bed. I look towards the window with the broken pane and through it I see the silhouettes of branches. They are rocking in the wind. I wonder if the blackbird sits amongst them, waiting to sing at the first hope of day. Like he does every day. I wish I had such a purpose in life.

In bed, leaning my back against the wall, I remember the wonderful feeling of friendship I felt this morning, waking on the sofa after an evening with Parker. How he'd helped me see some kind of light, some hope in my life. Peace. I think again of the time I heard him crying in the night, the first time he stayed. Now I realise it was me who was the guest, rather than him.

I feel I may not leave this house again. I have hardly any money, my job doesn't pay enough. I have Jessica and Eugene, but they know I'm broken. I see it in the way they look at me, in the way they check that I'm OK each day. I have no place to begin again from. I may not leave this house again.

There's no fire lit. I'm still wearing my clothes as I lie down and pull the blanket over me, covering my face. Again I hear the tick-tocks of the clock and the consuming silence between them. I can hardly keep my eyes open. I lie very still. I think, really think for a moment, whether I'm moving my arms or legs. I concentrate, suddenly awake and alert, like my life depends on it.

There's someone in the empty side of the bed.

FORTY-FIVE

I wake, slowly. My head is covered. I pull down the blankets and rub my eyes, feeling more ill than ever. There's a deep sickness within me. I sit up and look around. I'm not in my own bed. Under the blankets, I'm wearing only my jeans and socks.

This is not my room. On an old dressing table, there's a hairbrush, a shaving brush and aftershave, a shaped mirror on the back of the table and a little stool in front of it. There are posters of bands from the seventies on the walls. They're everywhere. Faded and yellowed. Jeans and T-shirts and underwear are strewn around the floor. They're not mine. I see the door is open and realise I'm in the locked room. I don't know how I've got here. This is not my room.

My phone is ringing. I look over the side of the bed. It's on the floor in the same place it would be if I was in my own bed upstairs. Eugene. I pick it up. It stops ringing and the last little bar of signal disappears. I remember, I'm supposed to be going for breakfast with Eugene today.

I go to the window and see that Blackheath has turned white. No snow falls now, but the heath is thickly covered.

Eugene is on the path outside, rubbing his gloved hands together. I feel I need to tell him, about Mia and Carl, the man on the webcam, about Parker and how much I'm afraid of this house now. I knock on the window, hard. It rattles in its frame.

Eugene looks up at me and waves. I wave back. Behind him I see the man sitting on the bench, looking at the heath. He sits in his usual position, watching over the unbroken early morning white of snowfall.

I begin to walk upstairs to find my trainers and T-shirt and coat, but after a few steps I hear a toilet flush. Slowly, I peer over the bannister, look up the landing, and at the end of it I see a door closing. The footsteps were too fast to have been Mrs Moore. I notice now that all of the doors, except that of the locked room, are closed. I continue up the stairs, quieter. I've never had this feeling that I'm sharing the house.

I reach the top of the stairs and I freeze. I hear the crackling of a fire. I stand very still, try to discover which room it's coming from and I realise it's the empty room, its door half open. I walk slowly down the landing, stand in front of it. I push the door gently and it creaks as it opens.

An older man with a brown beard sits beside the fireplace in a comfortable-looking chair, reading a book. He looks up, then back down at his book. The empty room has been filled: a single bed, wardrobe, boxes, folded clothes. Everywhere there is someone's life. Holly surrounds the fireplace, lit candles are on top of the mantel and wrapped presents sit beside it. I look back at the man.

'Who are you?' My voice has become a breathless whisper.

He just concentrates on his book.

I hear a noise downstairs and look over the bannister. A woman walks down to the ground floor, her shoes loud on the wooden steps. My bedroom door opens and I jump back, flat against the wall beside a grandfather clock that wasn't there before. A man walks along the landing. His chest is bare and he has a towel wrapped around his bottom half, his jet-black hair gelled back. He walks to the bathroom without acknowledging me, then slams the bathroom door closed. I hear the taps of the bath begin to run.

I go to the living room. The sofa has gone, but there's a single bed and a small table next to it. A wooden chair with flaky white paint. There are no boards nailed across the fireplace and a pile of grey ashes sit in the grate. Clothes hang on a rail. They're women's clothes, vintage, like Mia would buy from second-hand shops. A massive vase of flowers sits beside the fireplace. I breathe it deeply, the scent I've always smelled in this room. So familiar. It makes me feel I am home and my sickness is fading. I go to the window.

The view from up here is wonderful. The pathways across the heath have disappeared, only lines of black lampposts show where they were, and they're dusted with snow too. The pond has vanished in white, just a circle of long grass and bushes shows where it lies hidden. Everything has been silenced.

I bang my fists on the window. Eugene looks up at me, confused. I bang again, but he's not coming towards the house, so I leave the room.

The staircases and landing are decorated differently, more brightly, more alive. In the hallway, the door to Mrs Moore's basement flat is closed. I walk softly past it, wishing for the floorboards not to creak, and while looking down I see muddy paw prints leading from the front door, everywhere.

Just inside the door is a table, which I don't think was here before. On it sits a glass dome, antique-looking, lightly covered with dust. It looks like it had been sealed a hundred years ago. Maybe it's as old as this house. It looks stale inside, a block of space dead and locked in time, where a blackbird stands on a little branch. I look at him closely. He hasn't been stuffed very well. The feathers stick up on one side of his head, like he's been wearing a hat. I'm so relieved to see him. His still eye watches me as I move to the door and then open it.

I go outside. My footsteps are slow in the snow. I cross the road to the edge of the heath. The air is winter sharp.

'What the fuck are you doing?' Eugene says.

I'm so pleased he's here.

'Put a top on. You've got nothing on your feet!'

I grip his shoulders. I need balance, an anchor.

'Lewis, have you been drinking all night again?' He takes my hands, holds them.

I don't want to answer him.

I'm looking at the man on the bench. Parker is there, talking to him, as the man's hat nods slowly up and down. I've never seen Parker speaking to him before. It looks strange. Parker offers his hand and a woman stands. I see it's a woman now. There's a skirt showing from under the bottom of her mac. She wears small shoes. She's not dressed for snow.

'What the fuck are you doing, Lewis?'

Eugene is almost yelling at me now. His expression is stern, though I think he's more panicked than annoyed.

'You need to – oh, you're bleeding. Lewis, you're bleeding!'

He taps my neck a few times and I look at him.

'Lewis, your nose is bleeding bad, mate. We need to get you inside.'

He touches my face. As he takes his hand away, I see blood on his fingers. I look down. Streams of it run over my chest, splatter onto my jeans. Drops of it land in the snow, red burning white. The pain and sickness in my head has gone. A stupid dizziness has taken its place and it feels good.

Parker and the woman stand beside the bench now, facing me. He's speaking to her and pointing, but she's not looking at me and is disagreeing with Parker. She can't see me, but I can see her.

But it's not her.

I can't be.

Parker looks relaxed as always. He's reassuring her about something. Stamp stands next to him, his little legs hidden in the depth of the snow.

Eugene yells.

'Lewis, we need to get you to hospital.'

I hang in his arms for a moment.

The dull white sky is still full of snow. I feel snow against my back now, as warm blood streams down my face and neck. I turn my head, feel ice against my ear. Stamp looks at me, his little head leaning to one side in sympathy. I rub my forehead where I'd banged it when I crashed my car. I remember Stamp now, watching me from the other side of the road after I was pulled from the wreckage. Behind him, hundreds of birds are landing on the heath.

She looks so sad. I don't ever remember her being sad. Parker's still speaking to her. He's pointing at me again. She's squinting, trying to see something, until finally her eyes lock on mine and they widen. She's seen me. For the first time in nearly twenty years. She nods, tearfully. Aunt Ruth. I'm so pleased she's here.

I am free of everything.

Parker rests his arm on her shoulder. He looks at me, smiling. Does he know who I am? I want to call out and ask him, but then I realise. Of course he does. I'm drenched in the hope he's given me. He came to show me what I'd had.

I've loved.

I've seen it.

I've lived. He's shown me that now. I want to laugh, but I only choke and my eyes close. Eugene yells. I hear the front door of the house open. He yells again.

Mrs Moore is speaking to God.

A slap in the face makes my eyes open. I'm not sure which one of them it was. Mrs Moore or Eugene. Squatting, one each side, they look down at me, like they're peering into a deep hole.

'I've left my wife and everything's gone wrong.' It feels such a relief to tell them.

'Yeah, everyone's guessed, you dickhead.'

Mrs Moore glances at Eugene, her face recoiling, like she just smelled something bad. It makes me laugh.

And I do manage to laugh this time.

'You're going to be just fine,' Mrs Moore says.

'Sure he is,' Eugene says, as if it's never been in any doubt at all. 'But we're getting you to A&E to get you checked over.'

He helps me to my feet, and Mrs Moore walks ahead of us towards the house. She'll be heading for the kettle. I watch her old stocking-covered legs. They're slow and tired. But they still work.

'I think I hurt myself when I crashed my car. I banged my head.'

'When did you crash your car?'

'A few weeks ago.'

Eugene rolls his eyes.

He puts his arm around my shoulder as we cross the road to the house. At the top of the steps to the front door I stop, turn, and look at the snow-covered heath.

There's no one there. The snow around the bench is perfectly undisturbed. Even the birds aren't here now. I've always thought them to be the most guarded creatures. Elusive and lonely. The ones who don't tell.

'What are you looking at?' Eugene asks.

At the heath and into the white, where everything is ending and everything is beginning.

Acknowledgements

An enormous thank you to the ZenAzzurri writers, Anne, Annemarie, Elise, Jude, Nick, Oana, Richard and Roger, for feedback and guidance in writing this novel.

Thank you to Annemarie, Mandy and my sisters Michelle and Kathleen for readings and feedback on the early drafts.

Big thanks to Chris, Deepa, Harriet, Janet, Jo, Nathalie and Satinder, for our inspirational creative meets, over so many years.

I am very grateful to Elise for designing such a beautiful cover and for valuable advice.

Thank you to Richard for proofreading.

And thanks to my friend Joe, for our many, many conversations about how I could write this story, and others.

Made in the USA
Columbia, SC
08 September 2017